MW01075416

☒ LAZARUS

MAN

Books by John Lutz

LAZARUS MAN

BONEGRINDER

BUYER BEWARE

THE TRUTH OF THE MATTER

LAZARUS MAN

by John Lutz

WILLIAM MORROW AND COMPANY, INC.
New York *1979*

All characters in this book are fictitious and any resemblance to actual persons, living or dead, is purely coincidental.

Library of Congress Cataloging in Publication Data

Lutz, John (date)
Lazarus man.

I. Title.
PZ4.L977Laz [PS3562.U854] 813'.5'4 78-26967
ISBN 0-688-03468-3

Printed in the United States of America.

First Edition

1 2 3 4 5 6 7 8 9 10

FOR

BARBARA

☒ PROLOGUE AUGUST, 1974

PRESIDENT ANDREW H. BERWIN SAT like a thwarted, stern headmaster behind his desk in the White House. His face was haggard with the strain of the past year. In his small blue eyes glowed a rage suppressed to a defeated contempt. Despite his official aura, it seemed that at any moment his thin-lipped, downturned mouth would quaver with childish petulance. But he controlled his facial expression with a resolute, mechanical skill that did not quite deceive, like an aged actor who through dissolution has lost his touch.

Out of range of the single, stationary TV camera that seemed to nod at him in merciless scrutiny, stood his wife, his eldest daughter and Senate majority leader Warren Jennings. Berwin did not look at them as he concentrated on the task at hand, in the most difficult moment of his life.

On cue, he began his speech. He looked straight into the camera, spoke to his fellow Americans as if they were a small gathering on the other side of the room rather than 200 million people spread over thousands of miles. He recounted how during the past year his administration had come under increasingly vitriolic attack both from the news media and from certain political adversaries. The weapons: rumor, innuendo, and at times out-and-out lies. Though he had served honorably and accomplished much, the cumulative effect of the attacks on his administration had finally destroyed his ability to perform the duties of his office. It would be selfish and unfair of him to put the nation through another year of turmoil and uncertainty. There was a time to heal.

Effective at noon the next day, Andrew H. Berwin resigned his position as president of the United States.

☒ 1

☒ APRIL, 1980

WILSON CAPP WAS GRAYING. He was pallid. He was wiry. He was strong. Still strong. Four years in prison seemed not to have changed him but for a general sort of fading. And his eyes had resisted that fading. They were as alert and darkly intense as ever, perhaps even more so in contrast with the prison pallor of his gaunt, firm-featured face.

The face, which four years ago had gazed stoically from newspapers all over the world, was now even more inscrutable and uncompromising, the slightly crooked nose more pronounced, quizzical and pugnacious in its angle. A fortyish, handsome face, the sort of face one would hesitate peering into over the board of a serious game.

Capp had strictly adhered to a diet and exercise regimen in prison. The suit his wife had brought him fit perfectly, felt unbelievably luxurious and extravagant on him. He remembered buying the suit, a dark-blue medium-weight with vest, at Benson's five years ago. It had quickly become one of his favorites, and Myra remembered that. Capp gently nudged all thought of Myra to a cool recess at the back of his mind, as he had trained himself to do during the past four years.

Ahead of Capp loomed the familiar three-panel oak door. The door was opened for him, closed with an oiled, decisive click behind him. Receding footsteps.

He was alone with Warden Denninger.

Denninger, a large, blankly amiable-appearing man with uncooperative thinning blond hair, sat silently behind his desk with his hands folded awkwardly before him, as if posing for a press-release photo.

Capp stood easily, waiting for the warden to speak first, looking around and thinking as he often had how perfectly the office reflected the personality of its inhabitant. Windowless the office was, sloppy but impeccably clean, and, on close observation, with a well-used, convenient efficiency to its sloppiness. The dominant odor was that of pungent, cherry-sweetened pipe tobacco. The tobacco scent no longer bothered Capp; nine years ago, when he'd been sufficiently apprised of the physical hazards of smoking, he had quit abruptly and had never since even considered actually lighting another cigarette.

"Your day arrives," Warden Denninger said, finally giving in and breaking the intensifying silence.

Capp said nothing, buttoned his suit coat and stood staring at Denninger.

"I feel that we've stood by our promise to treat you like any other prisoner," Denninger said, unclasping his smooth hands. "I also feel that we've been fair."

"I've never complained."

"No. But then you aren't one to complain."

Capp stared calmly and unblinkingly at Denninger. He had hated the man from time to time during the past four years. But now he did not. He knew the hate had been only a visceral reaction to the imposed, absolute authority of Denninger's office. Possibly, in Denninger's place, Capp's behavior would have been similar to the warden's. The "fair" assessment, Capp had to admit, was accurate enough.

"These will be your last few minutes out of the limelight for a while," Denninger said. "They're waiting for you outside the gate."

"They," Capp knew, were the media. The media had been largely responsible for Capp's four years in prison. He held nothing against people doing their job. But he no longer had the patience to indulge the press, because intermixed with those reporters were others with personal or political axes to grind. They were the cause of Capp's disdain for the press in general.

There was, of course, no longer any reason for him to fear the newspapers; he had run his gauntlet and the press had lost its power over him.

"Worried about what I'm going to tell them?" he asked Denninger.

"Not if you tell them the truth."

"You'll find the truth can be worked like putty."

Denninger nodded, smiled. "I'll take your word for that."

"Are there any other formalities?"

"Formalities? No." Denninger stood and extended a large hand that seemed scrubbed to waxy lifelessness.

Capp shook the soft but powerful hand, and something between the two men seemed to dissipate. Now they were equal in the pecking order, if not within these walls, within society. Capp wondered if all outbound prisoners experienced that feeling.

Three firm knocks on the door. Then the door opened, and Myra was there, accompanied by a uniformed guard.

It was odd how different she appeared to Capp now that she was no longer separated from him by the visiting room's steel mesh: as if he'd suddenly encountered some exotic, elegant wild animal in the open, without the intervening bars of captivity.

But she was older: she had aged more than he had in the past four years. About her large, still-whimsical blue eyes were shaded crescents, and her features had perceptibly thickened. The faint flesh-sag and surrender of middle age that had somehow been hidden by the mesh of the visiting room was here plainly visible.

A sadness moved with a slow, gathering force through Capp. He fought it to an endurable dull ache. She had known from the beginning that they were part of the game, that something like this might happen. Their lives hinged on the imponderable.

Capp didn't move. Myra came to him without words and he hugged her to him. Her body felt unfamiliar and incredibly soft. The long-anticipated gut reaction didn't materialize. For a moment he was worried. Time, he thought. Time is the enemy, time is the friend. That part of it would be all right.

Myra looked up at him as if she wanted to say something, but she didn't speak. She smiled and stepped away from him, remained smiling. Denninger was smiling too.

"Goodbye and good luck, Wilson Capp."

Capp returned the smile and nodded. "Warden."

With Myra at his side, Capp moved toward the oak door and the guard came to life and opened it for them. The guard accompanied them down the hall, through Processing, along a gleaming tiled corridor of wavering images to wide steel double doors. Capp knew this was the remote Graham Street side of the prison. The heavy steel doors made a nice touch. Calculated?

The guard's nod was curt and perfunctory as he opened the doors for them. He'd played his part before; not his favorite scene.

They were there, as Denninger said they'd be.

The media.

Cameras clicked, whirred in the cool morning air. Voices rose, polite, persistent. "Mr. Capp, how does it feel? . . . Do you have any animosity? . . . How were you treated in prison? . . . How do you feel about Berwin's pardon? . . . What are your plans? . . ."

Capp said nothing, stood still above them on the prison's stone steps and stared over their heads at a distant hawk or small vulture wheeling effortlessly in the clear Kentucky sky. That high, beautiful freedom was largely illusory. Soaring birds depended on very real if invisible air currents.

"About Gateway . . . Mr. Capp? . . . Do you have a statement? . . . Sir? . . ."

Finally Capp lowered his eyes to look at his questioners. Sudden muted, hurried clicking and whirring of cameras. Sun glinting off lenses, eyeglasses; coattails and ties flapping in the morning breeze. Leather soles scraped the grit of hard cement.

"A broken bone mends stronger at the point of the break," Capp said simply. He stepped down to escort Myra to the waiting black Oldsmobile sedan that his lawyer, Bender, had provided. The TV and newspaper reporters, suddenly silent, instinctively fell back to clear a path for him. He opened the left rear door of the Oldsmobile for Myra and watched her gracefully lower herself into the car and slide across the seat to make room for him so he wouldn't have to walk around. He was vaguely aware of microphones being thrust at him, but thrust timorously.

"Mr. Capp? . . . What did you mean? . . ."

Capp took one backward glance at the neat brick walls of the prison, got into the car and slammed the door.

"My name's Larry Dellers," said the driver, a young curly-haired man with a sparse beard. "I work for your attorney, Mr. Bender." Sunlight glinted off a silver ballpoint pen tucked behind his right ear.

"Take us home," Myra said.

Dellers started the car and they pulled away, slowly at first. Faces peered in through the windows as Capp stared straight ahead. A left turn, speed, and the prison, the media, the grueling four years—it all dropped glimmering into the past. Myra rested her hand on his, cool and helium-light, as he settled into the plush maroon upholstery.

The interior of the Oldsmobile seemed opulent to Capp. Their acceleration was a subtle thrill.

☒ 2

When Raul Esteben read in the morning *Philadelphia Examiner* that Wilson Capp was to be released that day, he sensed a fine crack in the stifling structure of his present life. His days had taken on a dullness, a predictability and security that had become cloying. Now these things were perhaps nearing the end of their course. He smiled over his bitter black American coffee, a big man, with a deceptive layer of fat over hard muscle, with large, lustrous brown eyes whose gentleness like the smooth layer of body fat belied a hardness and will beneath.

"Capp was set free today," he said to his wife Marie, a small dark woman of subtle beauty and quick mannerisms. She was seated across from him at the round table, wearing a faded green housecoat, buttering a piece of crisp toast.

"It means nothing to us," Marie said.

"It means a great deal to me."

"Capp's a fool."

"He and I were fools together," Raul said. "He for his country, I for mine."

"But you're citizens of the same country."

"I'm not talking about the sort of citizenship represented by a piece of paper."

"Ah, but you'd feel differently if they decided to deport us to Cuba." Marie finished with the butter and laid her knife neatly across the rim of her plate, broke-tore her charred toast in half. A dab of butter she didn't know about clung stubbornly to the side of her right little finger, threatening to drop into her lap. Raul didn't tell her about the butter.

A warm morning breeze pressed its way into the apartment through the widely opened windows. The apartment wasn't air-conditioned: a window unit was an extra ten dollars a month. Since the loss of his government job and in the wake of his payment of the voracious legal fees, Raul couldn't afford the extra money. He worked nights now, teaching Spanish to adult classes at two neighborhood high schools, and the pay was less than adequate. It had soon become necessary for Marie to take her job as receptionist for a young, struggling dentist in the north end of town.

"I'd like you to promise me," Marie said, "that you won't become involved again with Capp. But knowing you, it would be useless."

"And unfair. Wilson Capp's a patriot. And you know he deserves my loyalty."

"You're *ciego*—blind! Capp made a thief of you, not a patriot."

"Anyone who even indirectly aids Cuba is my ally. I'm not a patriotic American; I'm a patriotic Cuban. That's what you won't understand."

"And what you won't understand is that you're now a naturalized citizen, an American. *Here* is where we live."

Yes, here, Raul thought, looking about at peeling paint, yellowed curtains and worn furniture. A crucifix hung crookedly on the wall above the sometimes-functioning TV, and Marie had added touches of red and bright blue throughout the apartment, as if to relieve the drabness of near-poverty.

It had been only slightly better in Matanzas, but it had been Cuba, home, where the heart lived. Marie didn't understand that. She also didn't understand that, like Capp, they were victims of betrayal.

What galled was that here the betrayers prospered, despite the minimal punishments they'd suffered. At home they would have been harshly dealt with; here they became rich, while those like Raul, the peons, were soon uninteresting to the media. But Raul knew it was unwise to underestimate the power of the peon as well as the power of the media. As Batista had discovered. As Berwin had learned.

"You lost your reputation and livelihood," Marie reminded him, "and two years of your life."

"I remember that every day."

"Then remember that what's right to men like you and Capp is wrong to others. That's why we're where we are."

"What's right or wrong is always arguable. That's why I prefer to follow orders. In certain situations it's right to follow orders. Always."

"Sweet Jesus, you'd think you'd learn." As she spoke, Marie waved her hands, and the glob of butter on her finger slipped to the second knuckle and barely held.

"Maybe I have learned." Raul's love for her was sometimes strained by his frustrating inability to make her understand. "Maybe in strength and consistency you see stubbornness and stupidity. When I left home, I learned what was important, and what was not."

Raul didn't admit to her the excitement of his work with Capp. He'd never even considered talking to her about that. It was a cause, something to do with that part of his life they couldn't force him to give up when he left Cuba. Years had passed, and the revolutionaries had become even more firmly entrenched beneath Castro. Then, with disconcerting quickness, more years had passed. Even Raul now had few illusions about the likelihood of a counterrevolution's imminent success. Possibly in his middle age he'd become a man who needed a cause. Possibly that was also true of Capp. In which case Marie would be right.

Marie bit noisily into her crisp toast with malicious force. "Are we more important than Cuba?"

"Objectively, realistically, no."

"Such a bastard."

"Some butter's about to drop into your lap."

☒ 3

Myra had directed Dellers to drive to an apartment she'd rented for the past four years, convenient to the prison. It was in a square, ivy-sheltered brick building in the small Kentucky town of Wesville. The house sat on a quiet blacktop street of a few similar buildings and shaded rows of large frame homes with wide, scrolled porches.

The apartment was modest, blue carpeting and drapes, slightly worn furniture, a portable black-and-white TV with a jumbled, silent picture. As Myra shut the door, a loud thump sounded from the apartment above.

It was unnecessary for her to live like this, Capp thought. She had access to the money from the lengthy and involved foreword he'd written in prison for *Masterpieces of Espionage*. The book had done well, mainly because of Capp's technically fascinating but personally unrevealing introduction.

Capp glanced around again at the apartment. Maybe this was the best Myra could do in Wesville. She'd told him while visiting in prison that it was a very small town.

Capp's attorney, Bender, was there, neat, dynamic, pin-striped and peppermint-scented, to shake his hand and congratulate him on his release. Bender's oversized, handsome gray head bobbed as a genuinely empathetic smile lighted his face.

Then the door to what Capp assumed was a bedroom opened. Bess, Capp's nineteen-year-old daughter, walked out, crossed the worn blue carpet and hugged him, jolting him a step backward with the force of her body. She was so much taller, so much more woman than girl. He was vaguely embarrassed when she kissed him. Time had made her a stranger.

Bess had been away at college much of the time Capp was in prison. He had seen her occasionally during the summers when she visited him with her mother. But again the thick steel mesh of the visiting room had been devious, had held back the years.

"I'm glad you're back, Daddy," she whispered close to his ear. A woman's voice, a woman's warm breath.

"You three want to be left alone," Bender said, beaming in reflected happiness. "I know I would." He shook hands again with Capp, then left the apartment, only to open the door a few minutes later and stick his Roman emperor's head in, now with a serious expression lowering his brow and the corners of his mouth.

"The press is downstairs," he said. "Don't worry, I'll deal with them. Unless you want to make a statement, Will."

Capp shook his head no, slipped an arm about Myra's waist, held hands with Bess. Bender nodded and closed the door. The air-conditioning unit clicked on with a low, vibrant hum that soon lost resonance.

Capp caught a distorted image in a corner of his vision, walked over and adjusted the rolling picture on the portable TV.

There was Bender, talking with over a dozen impatient reporters in the street in front of the apartment building. Capp smiled, a controlled, prison smile. Characteristically, Bender was enjoying the limelight. The diminutive, gray-haired lawyer was standing as tall as possible, head tilted back so that by the angle of his eyes he was looking down on the semicircle of reporters. Capp recognized some of the journalists from the crowd outside the prison gates. "No statement right now, gentlemen," Bender was saying with casual condescension. "Mr. Capp wants to be alone with his family for the rest of the day. And as you know, he seldom changes his mind."

Capp turned off the TV. Silence.

"Well . . ." Myra said, wedging the word into the silence.

Capp stood with his fists on his hips, looking around him. For the first time he noticed a square, chocolate-frosted cake with several unlit candles on it on a cloth-covered card table in a corner. In awkward white lettering on the cake were the words WELCOME HOME.

"I baked it," Bess said simply.

Capp smiled. A long time had passed since anyone had done a thing like that for him. "Why don't we have some?"

Bess went into the kitchen for plates and silverware. Capp could hear the discordant metallic jangling.

"Do you want a drink?" Myra asked.

"Not now." He could see that his answer had pleased Myra. During the interval between the end of the congressional hearings and the trial, Capp had drunk more than was his custom. Only a few times in his life had he drunk that much.

But with his conviction he had stopped drinking, gathering his strength for the time when his routine, hopeless appeal would be refused and he'd begin serving his sentence. Seven years, eligible for parole in four. Stiffer than the subsequent sentences of the others. But then Capp was the only one who hadn't talked, hadn't cooperated either with the committee or with the prosecution. He knew that the mills of the law had attempted to grind him exceedingly fine.

Bess reentered the living room with the silverware and dishes, then deftly touched a match flame to the seven candles on the cake. "Seven for luck," she said.

Capp grinned at his daughter, noticing that in various expressions and from certain angles she'd become a younger, prettier Myra, only with Capp's nose and dark intense eyes. "In a way, I suppose this is a birthday cake."

He walked to the cake and looked down at it for a long time. An impulse seized him, then was disregarded. He remembered a time when he had held his palm over a twisting candle flame to demonstrate his self-discipline, closing the door in his mind that could somehow disassociate him from the pain. Not now. There was no need to demonstrate his capabilities to himself or to anyone else. He knew that his time in prison had prepared him for what he needed to do.

Capp was suddenly aware of the intent expression on his face. Myra and Bess looked at each other. Bess started to speak but Myra shook her head no. Capp smiled and blew out the candles. He realized he'd forgotten to make a wish.

While Bess cut the cake, Capp walked to the curiously barless front window and looked down. The street before the apartment was now deserted. Bender had dealt effectively with the media—a particular knack that, if others had possessed it, would have precluded much grief.

The cake was delicious.

At four that afternoon, Bess left in a friend's new sports car to drive back to Jefferson University in Illinois.

Capp promised to visit her soon, then stood on the front steps of the apartment building and watched the tiny, insect-like green convertible disappear with an almost mystical quickness. Had the car been real? Had the long-haired girl driving it really been Bess? Capp felt a subtle uneasiness and glanced at the wristwatch they'd returned to him that morning, the gold Bulova he'd worn when he was admitted and forgotten about. Any second now, would the last bell ring with deafening command to signal return to quarters?

As if to beat the jarring clang of the bell, Capp abruptly turned and went back upstairs to join Myra.

She was standing at the small kitchen sink, scraping dark cake crumbs from the dishes into the garbage disposer. Capp walked to the sink and stood by her. The disposer slurped greedily, like a thing alive.

"That reminds me. I could use that drink," Capp said, trying a smile.

Myra continued scraping with the edge of a fork, motioning with her head toward the white metal cabinet. Capp opened the cabinet, rummaged behind some glasses and stacked Tupperware and found a full, sealed bottle of Seagram's V.O.

"Want anything?" he asked.

"Some of that in a Coke."

Capp opened the refrigerator for some ice, got glasses down from the cabinet and mixed Myra's drink, then poured straight whiskey over three ice cubes in the bottom of his own glass.

He set Myra's glass before her on the speckled Formica counter. "The house back east, what's its status?"

"All but three rooms and the kitchen are closed off. There's a young couple living in it. They'll look after it until we get back."

"Can you leave tomorrow?"

"I planned on it."

She turned off the sink tap and the whirring disposer and walked with Capp into the living room to sit on the threadbare sofa. A country-western tune was playing on a radio somewhere in the building, faint and forlorn: "I learned tooo love aaand lose aaalone . . ." Capp recognized the singer as a celebrity who garnered publicity from a long-ago stay in prison. "Aaa heart held innn walls of graaay stone . . ."

Myra was close to Capp. The older Myra, the different Myra, the same Myra. Capp took a sip of his drink. He knew he needed time for it to work. Christ, four years . . . Oh, Christ, the nights without her had left an ache and an emptiness! . . .

"What are you going to do about the future?" Myra asked.

"I have some ideas," he said, aware of the double-entendre. It was clear to Capp now how she had suffered through the years of their marriage. Not only had Myra not known about his future, she still didn't know half of what there was to know about his past. But she'd known he was in intelligence work when they were married; he'd obtained permission to tell her as much as possible and she'd known enough from her own involvement to understand how it might be. He reassured himself with that thought, but with the fresh perspective of the recently reborn, such comforting justification was difficult to hold.

The rules of the game were returning to Myra. She wasn't pushing him on the question other wives had every right to demand an answer to. She was sitting silently, sipping her drink in a parody of her old unassuming bemusement. Capp knew he owed her explanations impossible to give.

"While I sat four years in prison," he said, "the rest of them were cooperating with the committee or the prosecution. They were getting off with light or suspended sentences in return for their testimony, drawing nooses tighter around each other's necks, then making desperate deals to have the knots loosened. While I was supposed to be rotting in jail, they were granting interviews, writing books, lecturing, making money. Even those from before, from the Outfit, who knew the rules and violated them anyway to save their own skins. Stauker, Drake, Whitencroft . . ."

"I know the names, if little else."

"The talking had to stop somewhere. It stopped at me."

"Where else?"

"Would you have it another way?" Capp asked.

"I don't know. I honestly don't . . ."

Capp took another sip of his drink. It was Berwin who had caused it all, who had let the cancer spread. Capp had been proud to serve under Berwin, sincerely believing him to be the messiah the country needed. A president who was strong, honorable and unafraid to use secret, drastic means if the end justified them.

But it wasn't long before Capp noticed that the ends were not always honorable. Berwin merely sought what was expedient, and when a principle was no longer advantageous, he discarded it.

Then had come the Gateway fiasco, the refusal to admit culpability, and the throwing of subordinates to the wolves.

That publicly the President of the United States should deny involvement was one thing; that privately he should cooperate in condemning his most vulnerable and loyal servants was another. Berwin had thought himself safe at the pinnacle, and had let the structure of power crumble beneath him to crush those on the bottom. And other than Capp, all but those on the very bottom had become rich.

Even this small amount of liquor was making Capp slightly light-headed, relaxing him for the first time since his release. Maybe he was talking too much.

"All of them caved in," he said, "down to me and below, left me to dissipate or die in jail. Only I didn't. I saw to it that I grew stronger where they thought they'd broken me completely.

"And now?"

Now, they're my meat, Capp thought, but aloud he said, "Now finish your drink."

The country-western music had stopped and the apartment was quiet. Late-afternoon sun penetrated the closed blue drapes in angled, swirling lances of light, as if to illuminate choice objects: the closet door partly open to reveal the empty gray plastic arm of a raincoat, the dime-store print of Van Gogh's *Starry Night,* the overlapping moisture rings from glasses set without coasters on the glass-topped coffee table.

Myra was leaning against Capp and he turned to kiss her. She returned the kiss gently, and they put their glasses on the coffee table to add to the overlapping rings, stood and walked into the bedroom.

Myra undressed before Capp methodically, without the slightest sign of eagerness or apprehension. He found that without thinking about it he also was undressing.

Nude, they lay on the made bed. Myra had thickened about the waist and neck, and her breasts were larger, more pendulous than he recalled. It was as if in his long absence middle age had crept in to cohabit with her, to become her lover. They kissed then and time slipped and Capp knew that everything would be fine, that mentally and physically he would function as before.

With the kiss Myra seemed to give in to, then invite, the rush of long-suppressed passion; she gouged tapered fingernails into Capp's shoulder and arm, pulling him toward her with increasing force.

He mounted her, entered her, gently at first, unbelievingly. He felt her heart jump against him and heard the roar of his blood as he lost himself, began plunging in and out of her with a madly building rhythm, clutching her thickened buttocks with both desperate hands, hearing his distant harsh expulsions of breath as he crushed his shoulder into her cheek, driving her turned, uncomprehending face into the soft pillow. She was moaning something he couldn't understand, over and over. It didn't matter, didn't matter. God, nothing mattered . . . nothing . . . nothing . . .

He was finished with a suddenness that crashed him back to sanity. Beyond sanity, to heightened perception. From outside came the distant, singsong taunt of a child. The refrigerator in the kitchen was laboring with a persistent, watery hum, and something inside it, a bottle or jar, was singing a soft, wavering song against metal.

With exaggerated gentleness, Capp pulled away from Myra, out of her, and rolled to his side of the bed. The scent of her warmed flesh followed him. She was weeping. He resisted the vague anger he always felt in the presence of someone who cried.

Capp turned to her. "I'm sorry. I am. It . . . can be better next time."

But he wondered if it could.

Lying on her side, Myra propped herself up on one elbow, her breasts and stomach reddened from the violence of her union with Capp.

"Don't you think I know that?" she said, and kissed him.

He lay and watched the shadows move like a dark tide across the ceiling.

☒ 4

THE ROYAL-BLUE LINCOLN limousine carrying Helen Berwin to the airport pulled smoothly out of the circular driveway. Behind her stood the rambling pale beige stucco complex at Lost Palms, Florida. Andrew Berwin, one of three living former presidents of the United States, remained at the floor-to-ceiling window in his office. There he watched the sleek car slow at the first of two encircling patrolled fences, then wait while the Secret Service man worked the electrically operated chain link gate.

Helen, Berwin's wife of twenty-six years, was off on another of her trips, traveling semi-incognito as usual, without having informed her husband of her destination. Not that Berwin couldn't always get the information from Art Rapaport, the Secret Service agent in charge of the Berwin family's protection.

Berwin knew that Helen no longer cared for him; what love had existed had been displaced by a faint disappointment—more, a distaste. But for a thin public façade, Andrew Berwin and his wife were separated in every way short of duly recorded legal separation.

Berwin was a small man, with a slightly deformed carriage that was the result of polio in his early youth. He had saturnine if sagging features and wavy dark-brown hair, receding and combed straight back. Since his resignation under likelihood of impeachment, he had developed the nervous habit of frequently and quickly licking the left corner of his mouth, the tip of his tongue barely emerging, then darting back out of sight like a tiny animal testing the light. On another man this might have appeared ludicrous, but somehow not on Berwin. There was never any indication on his face that this unconscious act had occurred. His circled, intense blue eyes remained steady, strangely knowing and beseeching. An aura of tragedy overpowered any humor or lightness in his bearing.

The evening light was failing. Berwin could faintly hear the surf pounding the darkening sand beach on the other side of the complex. He closed heavy red drapes across his office window, cutting off the sound of the surf. Walking to his large walnut desk, he turned on the opaque-shaded lamp near his telephone. The bookcases along two walls, the long black leather sofa, the banks of polished wood file cabinets, all suddenly were softly shadowed, muted in form and substance. Gas logs in the fireplace flickered to hurl silent, flitting shadows over the deep red carpeting.

Berwin sat at his desk, knitted and unknitted his fingers. He picked up the remote-control unit for the large-screen TV mounted on the opposite wall and pressed buttons, studying the screen, trying to decide between banality and lies. He switched off the TV and decided that after dinner he'd watch again a tape of one of last season's Redskins football games.

After a while Berwin became aware of a soft drumming sound, then realized it was his own fingertips on the smooth desk top. In the void-like silence of the large office, the drumming sounded muffled, faraway and oddly solemn.

Berwin stood suddenly, walked to the wall behind his desk and opened a cabinet door. In a recess in the side of the cabinet, hidden by stacked volumes of the *Congressional Record*, was a telephone fed into a private line that even the Secret Service at Lost Palms didn't know about. The phone was a small white push-button model, with a coiled cord long enough to allow Berwin to talk seated in his desk chair. With darting, decisive jabs, he punched out a number direct and sat down with the phone.

"Alex?" Berwin said, when the phone was answered on the third ring.

Astounded, Alex Whitencroft recognized the precise, slightly hoarse voice. He'd never heard that voice on his apartment phone; he'd always called Berwin at prearranged times from public booths. "If my phone is tapped," he said, "they can trace the call back to you even if you don't speak your name."

"No," Berwin said, "I've taken care of that possibility."

"Of course," Whitencroft said, respect edging into his voice. For a moment he'd forgotten the lingering power of the man with whom he was talking. Whitencroft had been attorney general during the Berwin administration, and with occasional rare insight realized that the power of his own former office tended sometimes to keep him from regarding Berwin with the proper awe. They had, after all, been friends for years before Berwin's ill-fated presidency.

"What about California?" Berwin asked, getting to the purpose of his call.

"Up another three points in the Gallup poll, six points in the other polls. He looks like a winner, but it wouldn't hurt for something to happen to put him over the top."

"Nothing can be taken for granted, Alex. The polls aren't always accurate. Who conducts the polls? Who *writes* about the polls?"

"You don't have to remind me, sir."

Berwin searched the resonances of Whitencroft's "sir" for sarcasm, for hidden contempt, could find none. "What about your situation with the vultures?"

"I expect to lose my final appeal."

"I'd do anything I could. You know that, Alex."

"Of course. If there were anything practical to do."

"Things change, Alex, things change." Berwin could hear the note of loneliness in his own voice, wondered if its plaintive tone carried over the line. Did it matter? He and Whitencroft went back years, to the Chappaquiddick affair.

"Incidentally," Whitencroft said, "Wilson Capp was released this morning."

"And after years of legal maneuvering, you're about to be confined. Sometimes there appear to be advantages in being a small fish."

"He had fewer avenues of appeal than I had, though looking back on it the outcomes of our cases were predictable."

"You did what was natural; you have to fight them. They're bastards, Alex. You must never give in and play their game."

"Capp certainly didn't."

Berwin laughed a short, melodious throaty laugh. "He played his own foolish game. Capp was always a strange one. A man of extremes, but reliable. And uniquely competent in his job. What statement did he issue upon his release?"

"None, actually. A few terse meaningless words. I suggest you watch this evening's news. You'll enjoy seeing his method of dealing with the press."

"I'll do that, Alex. And I'll be in touch."

Without waiting for Whitencroft's goodbye, Berwin broke the connection, stood up and replaced the phone in its hidden recess. He glanced at his watch in the quiet dimness of his office and began to pace. The tip of his tongue made its instantaneous appearance at the left corner of his mouth. Pacing to the window, he opened the drapes, closed them, then went to his desk phone and lifted the receiver.

He punched a single illuminated button. "Hartwell, I'll be on the beach."

"Yes, sir."

Berwin walked from his office, locking the door behind him, and moved along a series of narrow, plushly carpeted halls. The walls and ceilings of the halls were white and unadorned. Berwin had them this way so they would create something of a maze, a minor but important final aspect of his security. And indeed first-time visitors to his office had to be guided along the short but confusing series of turns.

An outside door, guarded, a weathered flight of wooden steps, and Berwin was on the beach. He knew he was being observed. The Secret Service was there, invisible. They knew their job. He zipped his poplin jacket against the ocean breeze.

Berwin looked up with satisfaction at the canted half-moon, luxuriated in the pull of damp white Florida Gulf Coast sand beneath the soles of his shoes. The surf pounded with slow, metronomic force not ten feet from him, drawing back to sea to leave patterns of water boiling in the moonlight. Berwin knew that less than half a mile out to sea was a network of sensor devices to alert his protectors and prevent anyone's approach from that direction. He had little to fear from the sea; he had always loved the sea, the beach, the night sky.

He stopped walking and stared up at the engulfing blackness with its array of wavering yellow stars. Each tiny star seemed to pulsate as he stared, emitting forces that had traveled light-years, and he could almost feel a personal but universal power flow into him, infuse his body with strength, with will. A ponderous wave broke with a slapping crash on the beach, and fingers of tumultuous foam reached to within inches of Berwin's feet. He walked on.

He decided to return to the complex and watch the evening news as Whitencroft had suggested. His fists buried deep in his jacket pockets, his shoulders hunched, Berwin turned from the sea and headed in that direction.

After the network news he would watch a tape of the Washington-Dallas football game, the one pulled out by Washington in the final, desperate seconds. He needed to relax with a drink in front of the TV in his office, his very private office.

☒ 5

The telephone rang.

Only once.

Instantly Raul was awake and his hand darted to the bedside table to snatch up the receiver. "Yes," he said. A pause. He wriggled his nude body back carefully to sit up in bed. "Yes. Good. Here in Philadelphia. Enrico's on Twelfth and Gratton, three o'clock. Yes." He hung up.

Still with his bare back pressed against the cool headboard, he glanced at the glowing gold face of the clock on Marie's side of the bed.

Almost midnight. They could hear the occasional echoing whir of a car in the street below. A lonely, lingering sound.

"That was Capp," Marie said, unmoving, lying on her side and facing away from him.

"Yes," Raul admitted, slipping back beneath the lightweight sheet.

"*Ciego*!" Marie said in a very tired voice.

Raul rested a hand on the yielding roundness of her hip and went to sleep.

Enrico's was a restaurant and lounge, old, with shoulder-high oak partitions and widely spaced small round tables covered with red-and-white checked tablecloths. From the ceiling hung a great many viny green plants in round pots supported by triangles of converging brass chain.

Capp stood inside the door, spotted Raul at a table near a cascading plant with graceful pointed leaves and went to join him. A spicy, garlic scent seemed to warm the restaurant. Capp decided that the plants must thrive on it.

There were only a few other customers in Enrico's. Capp had chosen the time carefully.

Raul stood when he saw Capp approaching and grinned hugely. He did not proffer his hand until Capp's right hand was extended. The two men shook vigorously, Capp patted Raul's shoulders, and they were seated.

Capp saw that prison had left Raul relatively unchanged physically. Still the healthy dark complexion, even white teeth, alert brown eyes and hulking, powerful shoulders. If anything, Raul had put on several well-placed pounds.

A gray-haired waiter walked over to the table and stood expectantly. Raul had been drinking a stein of beer. Capp ordered V.O. and water.

"Have you been all right?" Capp asked, watching the waiter's retreating red-vested back.

"Me? Of course." Raul shrugged and took a sip of beer.

"Prison isn't jolly," Capp said, "even under the best of circumstances."

"I've been out more than two years. It's forgotten."

Capp knew better. Men like Raul who placed a premium on freedom never forgot prison.

The waiter came with Capp's drink and a fresh beer for Raul. Capp paid. He and his former subordinate lifted their glasses in a silent toast to both the past and the future.

"Have you seen Julian?" Capp asked. Julian Zayas, another Cuban refugee, had been their cohort on many important assignments. Including the Gateway Trust break-in, where by a fluke they had been discovered removing the contents of a U.S. senator's safety deposit box. Zayas was a lean, dapper man, perpetually smiling, handsome and seemingly nerveless. When at rest, he possessed a perfect stillness that Capp had noticed in many deadly men.

"I talked to him a few times on the phone," Raul said. "We received almost identical sentences, got out within a week of each other. He's well, in Cincinnati. But he's bitter."

Capp sipped his drink. "So might we all be."

"Bitterness corrodes."

"True. Action's preferable."

Raul tilted back his head and downed nearly half his beer. When he placed the stein on the table he was laughing. "My wife, she doesn't like you."

"I'm hurt," Capp said. "Marie's a beautiful woman, and sensible."

"It isn't personal. She's afraid you might get me into trouble again. She blames you unfairly."

"Not so unfairly. I recruited you."

Raul shrugged again. "Who knows what greater trouble I might have gotten into?"

The waiter had returned and was standing poised over them.

"Have you eaten?" Capp asked Raul. The big man nodded, declined Capp's offer of lunch. Capp opened a grease-stained menu and read quickly. "The tossed salad with house dressing," he said, "and a cup of black coffee."

"Marie's a perceptive woman," Raul said. "She knows it was you who phoned last night."

"I've always borne in mind Marie's perceptiveness. It's been a pain in the ass."

Raul said, "Whatever the job is this time, I've got to be extra careful. She's warned me."

"You haven't heard me out, and it sounds as if you're already agreeing."

"I am agreeing, Wilson, because I think I know what you're going to say. Like you, I've thought for a long time that something should be done. Vengeance."

"Not vengeance, justice." Even as he spoke the words, Capp was aware of their antiquity and power. Often misused words, not to be lightly applied. Coming from his lips, they had behind them years of deliberation.

Raul's broad features set in an uncompromising calm.

"Yes, we must administer justice, our particular kind of justice for our particular kind of people."

"Exactly," Capp said. "Marie's not the only perceptive member of your family." He was relieved. It had been easy, though he had never doubted that Raul would agree to help. "Do you know how I can get in touch with Zayas?"

"I thought you might want to, so I wrote down Julian's phone number." Raul drew a crinkled slip of white paper from his shirt pocket and handed it to Capp.

"You understand you'll be following my instructions?" Capp said, placing the paper in his own shirt pocket. He knew that loyalty and obedience ran like a tonic in Raul's soldier's blood.

"Of course, Wilson. Like before. And Julian will understand."

Capp saw the waiter arriving with his salad and quickly finished his drink.

The salad was excellent, the coffee strong.

"You must also believe, Raul, as I do, that what we're doing is necessary."

"It's our own kind who betrayed us to save their necks. They're the ones who in other countries would be stood against a wall and shot, not punished lightly and allowed to make money with accounts of their betrayals. To allow that kind of behavior is to encourage it. Good men die or go to prison, fates that differ only in their state of permanence."

Capp took a large bite of salad, chewed, swallowed and took a sip of coffee. At times Raul's philosophical strain bordered on rationalization and was damned annoying. There was no need for rationalization.

Capp said, "Raul, I want there to be no mistake about what I'm proposing."

"Execution."

"Unless we're caught. Then it would be murder."

Capp's conversation with Julian Zayas in Cincinnati the

next day went much as had his Philadelphia meeting with Raul. Julian had been looking forward to Capp's release, had in fact remained in the country in anticipation of a reunion with his former chief. The dapper, deadly little man owed Capp much and was eager to repay. He'd been a trained assassin in Castro's revolutionary force before defecting five years later to the United States. He was qualified.

Julian smiled most of the time Capp was explaining their purpose.

When Capp left Cincinnati it was raining, leaving vibrant horizontal streaks on the airliner's convex plexiglass windows. He slept after they'd gained altitude. When he awoke to the polite gentle prodding of a stewardess, he was near his destination and it was still raining.

No one was waiting for Capp at the airport. He claimed his luggage, a single large leather suitcase with a heavy brass lock, and walked to the puddled cement apron that was the taxi area beneath the main floor of the terminal building.

By the time he arrived home, in Washington's Green Hills subdivision, the rain stopped and the sky was a brightening mosaic of blue and gray. He stood before the two-story brick Colonial house and paid the cab driver. It was silly to keep a house this large. Since Bess had moved out and they no longer entertained, he and Myra could make do with an apartment. And they could use the equity from the house. Capp was amazed at how prices had risen during the past four years.

Myra was seated in a corner of the sofa with her legs crossed. She was wearing black knit slacks and a green sweater and was sipping a cup of tea. She smiled at him as he put down his scuffed suitcase in the hall and worked out of his coat. A few diminished raindrops flew and sparkled, flung by his coat as he tossed it onto a brass hall tree.

"Nice trip?"

"Fair," Capp said, returning the smile as he walked into the living room. She would never ask him where he'd been, why he'd gone. It was good to see Myra, to come home to her. Better than it had been since the early years of their marriage. Prison to thank for that, Capp thought wryly.

"Some tea?"

"Sounds just right."

Myra went into the kitchen, returned with a cup of tea. Capp sat on the sofa with her, removed his shoes and stretched out his legs. He hadn't traveled in a long while and had forgotten how tiring it could be. The tea was very hot, without cream or sugar, and very satisfying.

Light filtering through white sheer curtains lent the living room an airy, restful atmosphere that soothed Capp. The room was large, high-ceilinged, with pale-green walls, a green carpet and a white brick fireplace. On the mantel sat a hand-painted porcelain clock that marked the seconds with a measured, tranquil ticking.

"Have you given any thought to what we're going to do?" Myra asked.

"Do?"

"It's been lonely these last four years, Will. And when Bess left for college two years ago, it became almost unbearable. Loneliness seems to hollow out a person. The only small comfort I had was living in Wesville, in the same town as the prison."

"I had plenty of company," Capp said, "psychos, homosexuals and failed criminals."

Myra curled her legs beneath her, swiveled to face him on the sofa. "It's over now, and things can be good for us. We can make up for those four years. You can be free of the Outfit. In a way maybe it was all a blessing; it's the only way you'd ever have left them."

"It's a business you can never completely be free of, Myra. You know that from your own peripheral involvement. You just don't want to believe it."

"Gateway was unprecedented," Myra said. "You're a special case."

"It doesn't matter. Not to them, not to me."

Myra sighed. She finished her tea as if it suddenly had grown bitter. "Charles Drake phoned while you were gone."

"Drake? What did he want?"

"He said he read about your release and wanted to wish you well."

Capp grunted, retreated into his thoughts. Charles Drake had been legal counsel to the President during the Berwin administration. Twelve years before, he had also been a member of the Outfit. Because of Berwin's penchant for secrecy, many of those surrounding him had been former CIA members. Drake had long ago worked out of embassies in Paris and Copenhagen and had been involved in the 1969 Gordon defection and death. He was aware of the rules he'd broken, the significance of his betrayal.

"Did he leave a number?" Capp asked.

"He said he'd try to call back when you were here."

Capp nodded. Drake often had been referred to by his CIA colleagues as "the Weasel," both for his deviousness and for his refined but faintly rodentlike features. "Weasel" had even been his code name for several minor operations. During the Berwin administration Drake had been the first to make tenuous, self-serving contact with the Gateway investigative committee. Capp did not consider Drake's nickname at all inappropriate.

The phone jangled insistently, and Myra uncurled her body, rose and walked into the next room to answer it. Capp could hear her talking. It was a friendly, chatty call from the old woman who lived in the house behind them, concerning changes in the neighborhood, new shopping, new neighbors. None of it interested him even remotely.

Capp tuned out the mundane conversation and rested his head on the soft sofa back, closed his eyes and listened to the two-note measured ticking of the mantel clock. Drake was among those who had taken Capp's four years from him—six years, counting the tension and misery of the hearings and trials—taken the last of his youth, the last prime years of his marriage, the last of his daughter's childhood, taken his freedom. And there was Alanna . . .

Lukewarm tea found its way through Capp's pants leg onto his left thigh. He opened his eyes and saw that he'd tilted his teacup. There was a small oblong stain spreading on the coarse gray material of his pants. Moving nothing but his left hand and arm, he placed the cup and saucer on the table by the sofa and again closed his eyes. The warmth of the tea on his leg was not unpleasant.

He was sure of Myra, in every way. Despite what she'd said, she understood that he must retaliate for what had been done to him. Done to both of them.

☒ 6

Charles Drake phoned Capp at two the next afternoon and asked if he might drop by to see him. Capp said certainly, and Drake arrived at the Capp home at two thirty sharp. Like all of the former Outfit fraternity, he was routinely punctual.

Myra led Drake through the quiet entry hall and into the living room, smiling all the while and telling Drake that he looked very well and inquiring about his wife Laura. Laura was fine, how was Myra?

When Drake saw Capp he smiled nervously, faltering ever so slightly in his step. Myra excused herself and withdrew to the rear of the house as if she had some urgent need to go there.

Drake did look very well. He was wearing camel-colored slacks and a muted tan plaid sport coat. He was thin, but no thinner than before, and he seemed to have lost no more of his wispy light-brown hair. His glasses had slipped down slightly onto the bridge of his long nose, where they usually rode, causing Drake habitually to dart a nimble forefinger up to adjust them. He adroitly tapped his glasses to their proper position now and stared somewhat apprehensively at Capp with his watery blue eyes.

"You look much better than I thought you might," he said to Capp, stepping nearer and holding out a tentative hand.

Capp shook the hand, which was damp. As he stood gazing at Drake, he could see the slender, nervous man trying to read his eyes. Capp knew there would be nothing there.

"What brings you to Washington?" Capp asked. "Or are you living here?"

"No, I don't live here; I'm here to lecture at the university."

"For a fee?"

Drake seemed mildly taken aback. "Of course. Maybe it's something you should consider, Will. I mean, the lecture circuit."

"I'm not renowned as a talker."

"There's still plenty of interest, and we all have to live. It's a way of making lemonade out of the lemon."

Capp smiled. "Berwin used to talk like that."

"He talked too much, I'm afraid. And in the wrong places."

"He created the wrong places. The world's Berwins do."

Drake tapped his glasses and gave a faint grin, unable to disagree with Capp. He shifted his feet nervously on the green carpet. Capp noticed that he had on expensive tan dress boots with built-up heels.

"Why don't you sit down," Capp said. "I can have Myra mix us some drinks."

As he sat in the fruitwood chair opposite the sofa, Drake shook his head. "No, thanks. I have to get back to the university soon."

"What specifically is the subject of your lecture?" Capp asked as he settled into the sofa.

"Responsibility in government. In a perverse sort of way, I'm qualified to speak on that, you know." A hint of challenge in Drake's voice. "We all learned from what happened. If nothing else, we did learn."

The warm sunlight in the spacious room seemed to relax Drake. Now that he'd talked to Capp and faced the source of his apprehension, he felt that he could cope. From outside came the barely discernible swish of truck traffic on the highway. The ticking of the mantel clock was very loud.

"It wasn't too rough in prison, was it, Will?" Drake asked

hesitantly. "I mean, it wasn't like one of those South American hellholes."

"It was bearable."

"I admire you for what you did, I really do. We all should have stayed silent, but once it started it was impossible to stop. The committee knew what they were doing, knew how to apply pressure. The KGB could learn something from them."

"They learn from each other."

A nervous, quick laugh. Drake's thin, tanned face would be forever boyish. "Well, Ellson must have learned his lessons thoroughly, the way he ran the committee. Everything anybody told the old bastard he made into another brick, and you could almost see him walling you up, until you had to tell him something to make him stop. But he never stopped, only paused."

"You're a lawyer," Capp said. "You know how it works."

"I'm not a lawyer like Ellson. He's a syrupy-voiced predator."

"Berwin himself endorsed him to chair the committee."

The nervous laugh again, like typewriter keys striking in quick succession. "He had no choice, Will."

"I suppose not, at that point."

"Things get rolling, take on a life of their own." Drake drew a pack of Tareytons from his pocket, tamped one of the cigarettes on the side of a small gold lighter. After lighting the cigarette, he remained rotating the lighter smoothly and absently between thumb and forefinger of his right hand. "I wish I could have dealt with it the way you did. There's a residue of shame in the way I acted, the way a lot of us acted. The simple truth is we didn't have the guts. I mean, I've thought about it the past seven years, and when you boil away all the theorizing, all the moralizing and rationalization, that's what it comes down to, not having the guts. You were the only one."

Capp crossed his legs, clasped his hands over his right knee and leaned forward. "I appreciate you saying that, Charles. We're—we were—professionals, so it means something coming from you."

"It was simply fieldwork to you, wasn't it. That's something the public, even the committee, never understood. Another assignment. Tel Aviv, Berlin or Tennessee—all the same."

"The same."

"And maybe you're right, Will."

"What made you and Laura decide to stay in Baltimore?"

"We're not in Baltimore. Boston. We have an apartment with a view overlooking the harbor. On a clear day you can see the ships miles out."

"Family in Boston?" Capp asked.

"No, just some old friends. Actually, I travel almost half the time these days. I have an agent; he arranges my itinerary. You really should consider the lecture circuit, Will. Or a book. There comes a time when you can open up about certain things. You owe yourself that much out of the mess we stepped into. All of us owe ourselves at least that much."

"I suppose you're right, Charles, but I have a lot of thinking to do before I make any move at all. Prison sapped me of all my passions and drives. I'm hoping that in a few weeks or months I'll feel a bit more like doing something."

Drake shot him a hesitant, encouraging smile. "It will all come back to you eventually. You're not even forty-five, still a comparatively young man. At least we have that. Not like Whitencroft, who hasn't even begun to serve his term. All those appeals . . . sometimes I think it would have been better for all of us to plead guilty and get it over with. The outcome was inevitable."

"No outcome is inevitable."

Drake stopped rotating his lighter and looked curiously at Capp. "No, I suppose not."

"We can still rebuild our lives," Capp said. "It's just that right now I can't seem to muster the spark."

Glancing at his watch, Drake pocketed his gold lighter and stood. "I've got to get back," he said. "Two more lectures this week and then it's rest for a while." He moved toward the door and Capp stood and walked with him into the entry hall.

"Tell Myra goodbye for me," Drake said. "Tell her it was a pleasure seeing her." He sounded as if he meant it. He could sound as if he meant anything. That was his talent.

Capp nodded.

Drake opened the front door and turned. "I'm glad you feel this way," he said to Capp, "glad you came through it as well as you did. We all have to realize that it's in the past."

"The past is just that," Capp said, "the past."

They shook hands again. "If you decide you might like to lecture," Drake said, "I can arrange an appointment with my agent. The commissions they charge are pretty much standard."

"I'll think on it."

Drake nodded, started outside, then turned back again. "God damn it, Will, we go back more than a few years." The forefinger darted up to tap the glasses into place. "I just wanted to say . . . to let you know . . ."

"You've let me know." Capp reached out and touched his fingertips to the side of Drake's bent elbow.

Drake nodded, kept his head down, mumbled something about luck and walked toward the street without looking back.

Capp closed the door, went to the living room window and watched the elegantly thin lawyer get into a rented gray Chevrolet.

Drake sat motionless for a while behind the steering wheel, as if assessing the implications of his visit. Then he bent forward, a puff of vapor emerged from the Chevrolet's exhaust pipe and the car pulled smoothly away from the curb and accelerated down the winding street. It turned left and became a fleeting patch of gray between the houses at the far end of the block.

Myra was standing behind Capp.

"I heard him leave," she said. Capp knew she wouldn't ask about the content of their conversation.

He walked from the window and sat in the delicately worked chair used by Drake. "I'll probably have to go to Los Angeles in a few days," he said. "A business trip. I forgot to mention it to you yesterday."

Myra said, "I wonder about this boy Bess has been dating in college." She was staring out the upper part of the window. "He's a basketball player and was suspended from the team for breaking curfew." It was as if Capp hadn't mentioned a trip.

"Bess always had judgment beyond her years," Capp said. But he felt a tightening in his stomach. It was almost painful to think of Bess becoming serious with any boy. To Capp she was still fifteen, coltishly graceless and tentative in her actions. Nothing like the girl-woman he'd met in Myra's Wesville apartment.

Myra seemed to know what was going on in his mind, smiled at him remarkably like the way Drake had smiled at him ten minutes earlier.

"Going out for a while," he said. "Need anything?"

"Not at the moment," she said.

Capp drove from home to a large drugstore on Twentieth and Clark, the sort of place at which the dispensing of drugs is only a sideline to their real business of selling everything from jewelry to tenpenny nails. He passed the checkout counters and walked through Housewares and soft piped music to the phone booths near the back of the store.

Fishing in his pocket, Capp came up with some change to feed the phone and dialed the toll-free number of Holiday Inns. After making a reservation, he depressed the receiver button, stuffed quarters into the phone and dialed an area code, then Raul Esteben's number.

"Mr. H. will be at the Holiday Inn on Blossom Street in

Boston," he said, "Friday evening at eight."

He heard Raul Esteben say in a puzzled voice, "No one there," just before the click and buzz of a disconnected line.

Capp replaced the receiver, thumbed through the phone directory and stopped at the *Ws*. There were, he noted, over a dozen John Werners listed. He phoned Eastern Airlines and made a reservation under the name John Werner for a Friday-morning flight to Boston.

When he left the drugstore, Capp paused at the magazine rack and bought a *Newsweek* from the blond, acne-ravished girl at the end register. As he drove home he felt surprisingly cheerful, and he whistled a tune he hadn't thought of in years.

☒ 7

THE NEXT MORNING Capp drove through early rush-hour traffic to the Central Commercial Bank on Crescent Street. The morning was warm and dense fog had moved in during the night and stayed, wreaking havoc with the thousands of motorists trying not to be late for their jobs. If the sun didn't burn the fog away in another half hour, when the traffic rush really began in earnest, there would be a monumental snarl-up.

But the low orange sun made the temperature soar, and soon the fog had dissipated enough to allow good visibility even without headlights. Still, it took Capp more than an hour to cross town and park in the lot of the pale-stone mausoleumlike bank building.

Central Commercial didn't open until nine, so Capp went into a McDonald's across the street and ordered scrambled eggs, sausage and a large cup of black coffee. He sat in a booth by the window and leisurely read the morning paper while he ate. As usual, the world was in a hell of a shape but with room for decline.

Shortly after the bank opened, Capp crossed the street and entered.

Using the false identity with which he'd established himself at the bank, he gained access to his safety-deposit box. The box contained false identification he'd used over the years, driver's licenses from several states in several different names, credit cards, social security cards, passports, photographs of fictitious families, business cards, birth certificates.

Some of the dates were obsolete, but everything was of the highest quality and there were plenty of blank forms as yet undated. Capp selected what he'd need and left the bank to drive home and pack.

He took a cab to the airport, and in one of the many rest rooms he combed his hair in an uncharacteristic style down low on his forehead and put on a pair of glasses with dark frames and lenses of ordinary glass. Capp knew how to alter his appearance considerably with only the most subtle, natural touches, a skill that had more than once kept him alive.

Probably the precaution wasn't necessary. He doubted that anyone would positively recognize him by this time. But for the brief accounts of his release, he'd been out of the news too long to be deeply impressed on the public consciousness. Too many faces were thrust at people from TV, the newspapers and magazines, too many names, too many crises. Capp knew he had the advantage, too, of being a much larger man than he appeared to be in photographs. He suspected that at worst, if he hadn't taken his subtle, artful precaution, he might have attracted attention for his "similarity" to Wilson Capp. Now even that was unlikely.

He picked up his ticket as John Werner and boarded the DC-9 for Boston.

The flight was uncrowded, and Capp sat alone by a window and stared out at the marshmallow miles of cumulus clouds, marveling as he often did at their illusion of solidity.

There were no clouds by the time they reached Boston, only hazeless blue sky; the sort pilots and ballplayers call a high sky.

Capp used identification in the name of John Hollister to rent a car at Logan International, and he drove toward the Holiday Inn thinking about Charles Drake.

So the Weasel admired him and wanted Capp to understand that he was sorry for what had happened. Capp understood better than Drake suspected. What the Weasel said was probably true, but it wouldn't prevent him from behaving similarly in the future. And the price of the past had to be paid.

Capp wheeled the rented green Ford into the Holiday Inn lot and parked near the main entrance. After locking his luggage in the car, he went inside and registered, still using the name John Hollister, then got his luggage and went to his room.

The room was pleasant and quiet, furnished in motel modern, with a firm double bed and a color TV with a jumble of wires sprouting from its back. Walls and ceiling had been recently painted light beige. The tiled bathroom was clean, smelled of pine disinfectant and was supplied with plenty of towels.

As Capp walked back toward where his suitcase lay on the bed, he caught sight of himself in the mirror of the bare triple dresser and noticed how harmoniously he fit in with his surroundings. He'd spent the major part of his life in rooms like this, in various corners of the world. As if by some strange Darwinian adaptation, he seemed to have absorbed their anonymity.

Before leaving the airport, Capp had checked a Boston telephone directory and phoned down the list of Charles Drakes until he'd dialed the correct number. It was Laura who had answered the phone. Capp tried to persuade her to join a record club, but she wasn't interested. He hung up on Laura and memorized the Drakes' address from the airport phone directory. After unpacking his suitcase, he left his motel room and drove there.

The address turned out to be that of the Crowder Arms on Crowder Avenue, just off the Fitzgerald Expressway and not far from the Federal Reserve Bank. It was a sky-probing, needlelike building that fit not at all the ideal of aged and proper Bostonian architecture. As Capp turned left onto

Crowder and drove slowly past, he was disappointed to see that the building employed a doorman, a quasi-military figure in smart pale blue.

Across the street from the Crowder Arms' fringed canopy and burnished double doors were a bay-windowed boutique, a shoe store and, farther down toward the corner, a public phone booth next to a bus stop with a sheltered bench. Another tall building, the Belcrest Arms, was situated on the opposite corner.

Capp parked the Ford down the street, scribbled something on a scrap of paper and walked back toward the Crowder Arms. He entered the small, cork-floored lobby and stood before the brass bank of mail slots, pretending not to notice the blue-uniformed doorman near the elevators. Capp immediately found the Drakes, 27-B, but he was looking for something more.

"Can I help you, sir?" The doorman was suddenly beside him, an elderly, heavyset man with a kind, florid face and a no-nonsense bearing.

"Simpson, 20-C," Capp said, still studying the bank of names.

"No Simpson here, sir."

"Must be."

"I'm sure there isn't, sir."

Capp drew the paper he'd scribbled on from his pocket and showed it to the doorman, who adjusted his visored cap and studied the writing with interest.

"This says Belcrest Arms, sir. This is the Crowder."

Capp looked disbelieving, then stunned, as he took the paper from the doorman's sausage fingers and examined it. He groaned and glanced at his watch.

"The Belcrest is right down the street, sir."

Capp appeared relieved. "How far down?"

"Next block, on the corner." The doorman pointed to demonstrate which direction Capp should walk.

Capp thanked him and hurried out.

When Capp reached his car, he jotted down the four names and apartment numbers he'd memorized, all women's names. Then he drove down the street, turned into the Crowder Arms parking lot and circled slowly as if seeking a parking space. The parking slots were marked in yellow paint with apartment numbers, and he made notes of models and license numbers of parked cars that corresponded with three of the women's names. The fourth slot was empty. Satisfied, Capp returned to the Holiday Inn.

After a shower and change of clothes, Capp had the rib-eye special at a small steak house he'd seen near the motel. Then he drove to a supermarket and bought a fifth of bourbon and returned to his room to wait for Raul and Julian. He was totally confident that his plan would work. It was time to begin calling in the debts of those who owed.

The next morning Capp was parked where he could watch the Crowder Arms' lot.

At 7:45 A.M. a slender, elderly woman in a fur-collared sweater walked across the lot and got into a yellow Pinto. According to the information Capp had compiled yesterday, that would be Adelle Klein, 16-C. Capp watched her drive from the lot, probably on her way to work.

Ten minutes later a rather pretty, thirtyish redhead crossed the lot and with a great show of leg got into a green Volkswagen Beetle. She was carrying what looked like a large leather artist's portfolio. Capp made a tiny check opposite her name, Helen Eustace, 29-C, two floors above the Drakes.

It was 8:30 A.M. when Marjorie Repetto, 14-A, emerged from the Crowder Arms. She was a middle-aged woman, dark-haired and extremely attractive. A man was talking to her, his arm casually encircling her waist. The man was tall and blond, wearing a gray vested suit and carrying an attaché case. The couple lowered themselves into Marjorie Repetto's red Corvette and drove away.

Capp left to get some breakfast, then he drove to a florist's shop and bought a dozen long-stemmed roses. On a card he carefully printed, "In the hope that you'll return my affection —your most ardent admirer." He took the roses with him, in a long white box lined with tissue.

By three that afternoon the green Volkswagen had returned. Capp had been hoping for the red Corvette, but the Volkswagen would do.

At 3:15 P.M. Julian Zayas, wearing a nondescript white delivery uniform, approached the Crowder Arms' doorman and explained that he had flowers for Helen Eustace in 29-C. The doorman buzzed Helen Eustace and told her about the flowers, and she said in a faintly puzzled tone that it was all right to send them up. Julian tucked the roses beneath his arm and walked to the elevators.

Helen Eustace was thrilled. She tipped a dollar.

Before returning to the lobby, Julian detoured by way of the twenty-seventh floor, located the Drake apartment and committed the layout of the upstairs Crowder Arms to memory.

Charles Drake sat down across the table from his wife Laura the next morning to a breakfast of poached eggs, orange juice and coffee. The *Boston Globe* had been left outside their door, and Laura had laid it folded on the table beside Drake's plate.

Drake probed with his fork to see if his egg was firm enough and glanced at the bold black typeface of the folded newspaper.

He took a bite of egg. "The Middle East again," he said. "That's all they seem to write about."

"I can remember what they wrote about before," Laura said. "You should know how the Middle East feels." She was smiling as she lifted her coffee cup.

Now in her late thirties, Laura Drake was as attractive as when she'd appeared on the televised committee hearings, seated placidly behind her husband and lending him a calm and almost regal support. She was a serenely appealing woman, with a round, radiant face like a tranquil full moon, one of the few women Drake had known whose beauty actually was enhanced by a straight, severely skinned-back hairdo.

Drake finished his egg quickly and turned the paper to the section containing the daily horoscope. He knew it was absurd for a man of his practical background to read his horoscope, but somehow he'd formed the habit. Almost invariably the horoscope was favorable. Maybe that was why he read it every morning. For so long everything he'd read applying to him in a newspaper was unfavorable.

"'An old acquaintance will lend a helping hand today,'" he read aloud, adjusting his glasses. "'And problems of an inconsequential but nagging nature will suddenly be solved.'"

Laura, who was even more practical than her husband, ignored him and swished her coffee about in her translucent white china cup. Her egg and buttered toast lay untouched before her. She usually had no appetite for breakfast. "I often wonder what the public really thinks about it," she said, "the way most of the influential Gateway participants came out of it with light or nonexistent sentences."

"Oh, the public knows there's a double standard; they're willing to accept it even though they don't like it, because the majority are uninvolved and see themselves only as spectators."

"Royalties out of the rubble," Laura murmured into her cup.

"That's good." Drake laid down the paper. "You ought to send it in to the *Washington Post.*"

Laura smiled. "We wouldn't want public reaction stirred up now."

"It's private reaction I've been wondering about," Drake said, but Laura was no longer listening. She'd stood up and was walking to the window to gaze out and check the weather. She had rather thick but shapely ankles and a graceful, slightly pigeon-toed walk that suggested she had been a dancer, though she had never danced. Drake sat at the table and watched the elegant roll of her hips beneath the material of her yellow silk robe.

"Are we going to Robbie's cocktail party tonight?" she asked, looking out at a cloudless sky and a pollution-haze-enlarged sun that suggested warmth.

"I told him we'd be there."

"I'll have to buy some comfortable shoes if I'm going to be standing all that time."

"Buy something expensive and sexy," Drake said. He knew she secretly hated Robbie's parties and was happy to indulge her.

"Sexy isn't for cocktail parties. Clumpy, soft, fat pods you can conceal with a long dress are for cocktail parties." She went into the bedroom to dress.

Drake got up from the table and carried the newspaper to a comfortable chair in the morning light. He sat down, propped up his slippered feet on an ottoman and turned to the editorial page.

Ten minutes later Laura, now wearing a tailored mauve pants suit, walked to the entry hall closet and got out her purse and a light coat to carry over her arm.

"Want anything while I'm out?" she asked.

Drake peered around his paper and shook his head no, wiggled three fingers of his right hand in a goodbye wave as he heard the apartment door open and close. He finished Jack Anderson's column, set the paper aside and got up to shower, shave and dress.

In the bathroom off the main bedroom, Drake bent over the large tiled sunken tub and worked the chrome handles of the shower, turning the water on full blast so it would be hot when he stepped inside the frosted-glass sliding doors. Then he walked into the bedroom, laid out some clean underwear and socks on the bed and removed his bathrobe and slippers. Nude, he returned to the bathroom to shower.

He slid open one of the shower doors, deftly adjusted the faucets so the water wasn't quite scalding, then stepped down into the wide blue-tiled sunken tub. Closing the sliding door, he stood directly under the pulsating hot spray of the shower head, letting the needles of water sting and the rising steam engulf and relax him.

Outside, across Crowder Avenue, Raul Esteben watched Laura Drake give the Crowder Arms doorman a polite if distant smile and get into a cab. When the cab had driven away, Raul walked the short distance to the phone booths on the corner, went inside one of the booths and dialed a number. After a brief conversation, he walked just far enough up the street to be able to see the entrance of the Crowder Arms. He glanced at his watch as if waiting for someone, then pretended to study the display of boots in the shoe store window.

The Crowder Arms doorman looked up from his morning crossword puzzle to see the same slender, Latin-type deliveryman who'd been there yesterday.

"Flowers for Helen Eustace, 29-C," Julian said. He held the long fragile box containing more long-stemmed roses carefully beneath his right arm. The unsigned card inside read "Still your most ardent admirer."

The doorman raised an eyebrow in a curiously Germanic manner. "You were here before, right?"

"Yesterday. It looks like somebody is hot for Helen Eustace."

Julian thought that perhaps he and the doorman would exchange some gossip about the Eustace woman, but instead the doorman walked to the row of intercom buttons and informed 29-C that more flowers were on the way up.

It took Julian less than five minutes to deliver the roses to their pleased recipient. She tipped him another dollar. He thanked her, walked to the end of the hall and got into the same elevator in which he'd ridden up. He punched the button for the twenty-seventh floor.

Julian had filed the bottom of his Visa card to a fine edge.

The lock on the Drake apartment door was exactly like the lock on the Eustace apartment, and he had no trouble using the card to slip it and silently step inside. As he quietly closed the apartment door he stood listening, his head inclined to one side and his body lightly poised.

In an instant he recognized the sound of the running shower and realized its source. He walked toward the sound, into the bedroom. The bathroom door was partly open, emitting bright light and the constant drum roll of the shower.

Julian quickly removed his shoes and socks, peeled off his white delivery uniform and his underwear, folded everything neatly and laid it on the bed beside Drake's clean underwear and socks.

He entered the bathroom and without hesitation drew back the sliding glass door and stepped beneath the shower with the astounded Drake.

Drake stood wide-eyed, a large bar of green soap in his right hand. There was more steam in the shower than Julian had anticipated, more heat. Julian saw that Drake's penis was shriveled and very small and knew the condition was the result of fright. Not a full second passed before Julian skillfully placed a leg behind the paralyzed Drake's knee and with the palm of his hand against Drake's chest levered him to the base of the wide sunken tub.

The swiftness of his descent left Drake momentarily stunned. With amazing speed, Julian gripped Drake's head, tensed lean arm and shoulder muscles and cracked the back of Drake's skull against the tiled edge of the tub. The motion was deft and decisive, accomplished with the sort of flourish a master chef might display in the breaking of an egg.

Julian stepped out of the shower just before pinkish diluted blood began to swirl about the base of the tub toward the drain.

As he closed the glass door by its chrome frame, he briefly admired the sunken tub with its mosaic of tiled flowers. It would be an enjoyable place to be with a woman, he thought, smiling for a moment as he remembered Laura Drake as she'd appeared during the televised committee hearings. He wiped his fingerprints from the shower door with a towel and used the same towel to dry himself.

In the bedroom, Julian dressed quickly and without wasted motion. Then he folded the damp towel he'd used and placed it in a pocket. He left the same way he had entered, locking the apartment door behind him.

☒ 8

FORMER DIRECTOR OF DOMESTIC AFFAIRS Mark Haggar sat alone in his study, sipping port on the rocks and watching the small Sony color TV on the bookcase near the door. He was watching the CBS evening news, waiting for the report on Charles Drake's death, while with another part of his mind he was listening to his daily maid Nora moving about in the other rooms of the apartment.

Haggar was a small man who, if he wasn't careful, had a tendency to put on a great deal of weight about his middle. He had a chiseled-featured but flesh-padded face dominated by quick dark eyes, and he had an almost perfectly circular half-dollar-size bald spot on the crown of his head that had stayed exactly that size for the past twenty years. Haggar was fifty now, and relying more and more on health foods and current diet programs. He ate only dark breads, used artificial sweeteners without saccharin and jogged three miles at least twice a week. He was still overweight.

He sipped his port and leaned forward in his modern leather-and-chrome chair as he heard the newscaster mention Drake's name.

Nora chose that moment to plug in the vacuum cleaner in the next room. The TV picture became a jumble of dancing, jagged horizontal colored lines.

Haggar leaped from his chair, slopping port over the rim of his glass onto his hand, and took three long steps to the door.

"Nora!" He saw that the port had stained his cuff.

The passive, square-shouldered old woman didn't hear him above the whir of the vacuum cleaner she was studiously pushing over the gray carpet.

Haggar yelled louder and she started, glanced imperiously at him and flipped the switch on the vacuum cleaner's curved handle.

"There's something I particularly want to see on the TV," he told her as patiently as possible. "The vacuum-cleaner motor interferes with the reception. Do you mind waiting a moment?" Without allowing her time to answer, he moved back inside the study and found himself looking at a buck-toothed housewife in a state of orgasmic pleasure over a new brand of peanut butter.

Nora sidled into the cozy study behind him, looked at the TV screen, then looked at Haggar. She'd come in daily to clean for Haggar for the past three years and took certain liberties. Theirs was a festering love-hate relationship.

"Is it vitamin-enriched?" she asked.

Startled by her presence, Haggar turned. "What?"

"The peanut butter. Is it vitamin-enriched? Is that why you're interested in it?"

Haggar didn't answer as the delirious housewife was replaced on the screen by the professionally groomed and somber network news anchorman.

"I'll dust until the next commercial," Nora said, and shuffled from the room when Haggar ignored her in his concentration on the news.

Haggar had heard an earlier radio bulletin about Drake's death, but it was details he wanted. Drake's body had been discovered too late for the story to be in the evening papers.

Laura had found Drake, having returned to their apartment at 3:30 P.M. from shopping and a luncheon engagement. But she had phoned home at noon and received no answer. The medical examiner had fixed the time of death at approximately 9 A.M., shortly after Laura had left to shop.

Drake had apparently slipped while taking a shower and

struck his head. There was no reason at this point to suspect foul play.

There were some shots of Drake's apartment building in Boston, and some grim footage of the sheet-wrapped body being removed and placed in a city ambulance. A quick montage, then: the apartment building again; Laura sobbing with a sort of calm acceptance and smoothing back her hair; several unsmiling police officials in coats and ties; the ambulance and a police car driving away with red dome lights flashing. Haggar knew it would take days for the details of the death to be made public.

"Okay to sweep now?" Nora asked. She had returned and been standing inside the doorway.

Haggar nodded, continuing to stare at the TV and sipping his drink.

"It's terrible about Mr. Drake. You knew him well . . . I mean personal, didn't you?"

"We were close acquaintances at one time."

"Well, it's awful. He was still a young man. You sure never know." She disappeared again and the vacuum cleaner began its drawn-out, frantic whine.

When Nora had left, Haggar turned off the TV, sat at his desk and phoned David Wellman.

Wellman had been director of White House operations during Berwin's administration. He'd been one of the most despised men in Washington, a smiling but devious buffer for the President. Wellman and Haggar had become friends after Wellman put in a word with the President and had a minor bureaucratic rival of Haggar's ousted from the Commerce Department.

Like Haggar, Wellman was single, but divorced rather than a widower. He lived alone in an unremarkable apartment where he was working on the manuscript of the book that was to restore his fortune.

"Wellman," he said simply as he answered the phone.

"David, this is Mark. How's the book going?"

"Tediously," Wellman said. "And the damned characters won't behave the way I want them to." Something in Wellman's tone suggested that he might have an easier time getting flesh-and-blood characters to behave more to his liking. That was a different sort of art he'd already mastered.

"Have you heard about Drake?" Haggar asked.

"Yes. A shame. But I can't feel a great deal of sorrow. Remember, he's the one who punched the first hole in the boat. I sent some flowers this evening."

Haggar phrased his next question carefully. He didn't want to put any ideas in Wellman's mind. "What do you think about . . . the way he died?"

"Most accidents happen in the home," Wellman said with a somehow gloating irony.

"Then you see it as an accident?"

"How else? James Bond is as dead as Drake."

Haggar crossed his ankles, rotated back and forth gently in his swivel chair as if the toy of shifting winds. "Have you ever thought about the lack of reaction to what happened during the Berwin administration?"

"Seems to me there was a hell of a lot of reaction. Or do you mean public reaction?"

"I mean public," Haggar said. "There was never any public *outcry*, no rage, no catharsis."

"I've thought about that," Wellman responded. "It simply reinforces my belief that most intelligent people in our position might have behaved similarly. They understood and got on with their lives."

"But what about the minority who for one reason or another aren't willing to forget? There must be a vast number of them out there. It almost seems logical that somebody, some crackpot, would take things into his own hands."

After a pause Wellman said, "You're saying you think Drake was murdered?"

"No, no, but I am considering the possibility. I suppose that all these years I've been waiting for something like this to happen. Remember some of the things printed about us in the papers, discussed on TV and radio. Out of the millions out there it would take only one twisted mind, one finger on a trigger."

"Drake wasn't shot, he fell in the shower and hit his head." There was a tight exasperation in Wellman's smooth voice. "Surely you didn't expect all of us to outlive our contemporaries."

"Suppose then if Drake was murdered it was by a professional, made to appear accidental. Some of our old running mates as well as others in the business were hurt by what happened."

"Are you thinking of Stauker?" Wellman asked.

"Or Wilson Capp, maybe some of the Cuban expatriates," Haggar said.

"But they were hurt for the same reason we were—because they were involved. And the Cubans were only soldiers; none of them saw the whole cloth."

"None of them that we know of. And Capp and Stauker, you know their records."

Wellman quickly agreed. "And I know that a lot of records were obtained after the fact. As in the case of Berwin's war medals. He was running for President even then. Every time he blew his nose and it bled, he made a note of it, and later his connection back home saw to it that he got a medal."

"Stauker and Capp were the genuine articles, though," Haggar interjected. "I recall a rumor of twenty years ago that Capp was such a fanatic he was willing to let himself be turned over to the Russians in some farfetched double-double game."

"I remember that rumor. I didn't believe it then and I don't now." A soothing quality took any hint of an edge from Wellman's tone. "Drake slipped in the shower, that's all. Tomorrow I might get struck by lightning. It's that kind of shitty world."

"I never enjoyed being caught by surprise," Haggar said.

"But that never kept it from happening. At least not one hundred percent. For the sake of argument, consider Stauker and Capp. Stauker is a much-mellowed man since his wife died. Besides, he's involved in Lazarus. And Capp is maintaining his macho superspy image, no doubt for its commercial appeal. The foremost thing on his mind probably is potential future royalties."

"What about the possibility of Drake's death being connected with Lazarus?" Haggar asked.

"Highly unlikely, since Lazarus doesn't involve Drake."

"I suppose you're right," Haggar said uncertainly, "but we're all linked in the public mind. Are you attending the funeral?"

"That would appear hypocritical. I've already sent my condolences to Laura."

"That seems the proper touch," Haggar said.

"Keep that imagination in check," Wellman said kindly.

Haggar said that he would and before hanging up told Wellman to take care of himself. Only after replacing the receiver did Haggar realize that his parting words might have sounded ludicrous.

Haggar sat quietly and thought back to the afternoon, when he'd first heard the news bulletin announcing Drake's death. Fear had crept in on him, a fear he'd refused to acknowledge. That had been the secret of his survival years before in the Berlin office, not acknowledging his fear. He hadn't been cut out for that kind of work. His heart was weak, his nerves tautly strung. If he'd been a field agent he would never have made it.

He reached for a meerschaum pipe in the circular rack on his desk. The pipe smoker's ritual of packing and firing up always relaxed Haggar. Once a three-pack-a-day cigarette smoker, he had switched to a pipe and used a specially blended low-tar tobacco. When the meerschaum was stocked up and drawing smoothly, he stood and walked into the next room.

Haggar stood at the wide sliding glass panel that led to his small iron balcony and stared out at the bright, sloping galaxy of city lights below. The view was panoramic, and it occurred to Haggar that there were many thousands of people below who, if they knew where to look searchingly, could see the yellowish frame of light he stood in. Haggar was vulnerable; everyone really was. It would take only one of that vast number below with a compulsion to murder in his or her twisted mentality.

Considering Haggar's notoriety, his misrepresentation in the press, the festering public knowledge of a double standard of justice, was it so unlikely that finally such an assassin was out there?

☒ 9

ASSASSINS CAME TO Oberammergau, Germany, during the sixties, and left shortly thereafter more proficient at their trade.

Oberammergau is a small, picture-postcard city some seventy-five kilometers south-southwest of Munich. In most ways it is an unremarkable city of good drink, good food and open Bavarian friendliness. In most ways.

The function of the CIA "special school" located there was much more than to sharpen those skills necessary to successful political assassination. Which was why in the summer of 1960 Wilson Capp was attending the school to have impressed on his mind in as brief a time as possible the nuances of central Russian dialect and physical mannerism.

The summer had been mild, with a cool and capricious breeze off the Tirolese Alps. And that playful, questing breeze found its way through the open window of the cool green room where Wilson Capp was tolerating the persistent corrections of one of his instructors, Alanna Hamner, an English girl who had grown up in Russia.

Alanna was a tall blonde in her early twenties. She had an incredibly lean waist, oversized graceful hands, faintly hunched shoulders and a cream-complexioned face that was almost impossibly angelic. She had been with the Outfit five years, and Capp knew that some time ago she had at great personal risk furnished hard information concerning the planting of sophisticated listening devices within the walls of both the English and American embassies in Moscow. It had been necessary for her to seduce and then kill a

Russian agent in order to accomplish this feat.

Capp was in love with her.

He hadn't, of course, planned on being in love with Alanna, and initially would never have predicted it.

During their first lesson she'd been ruthless and impatient, driving Capp to retain unconnected trivia that had no apparent bearing on his task.

Then two nights later he had seen her in a small beer garden in Ruppet Allee. Her demeanor there was completely different from how it had been at the school. She was smiling often and openly flirting with two appreciative young coffee-sipping Polizei cadets seated in a nearby booth. If she saw Capp drinking a bourbon at a table near a colorful elevated flower bed, she gave no sign. When she left alone, he followed.

All the while he was behind Alanna she was seemingly unaware of him. But when she reached the small flat where she lived, she stopped outside the gate, turned and stood waiting for him.

"Come up," she said unsmilingly as he approached. She might have been only slightly drunk.

As Capp followed her through an ornately carved doorway and up steep, narrow steps, she didn't glance back at him. She dug noisily in her large leather purse for her key. The place they were in smelled as if someone were cooking something in dark beer, and the aroma was mingled with the faint lilac fragrance of Alanna's perfume.

Capp spent the night there. And the next several nights.

The Outfit almost certainly knew about their relationship, though nothing was ever mentioned to either of them. And it never occurred to them until much later that their relationship was intended. The beer garden had been suggested to each of them. And at a later date Alanna was to be interrogated about Capp's most intimate beliefs and psychological undertones. Only years later did they perceive the design.

"Not that way at all," Alanna said sharply, as the cool

breeze ruffled the papers on her desk. "While a Russian from near the Siberian border might merely stand with his arms crossed, he is also apt to press his fingertips beneath his biceps, near the warmth of the armpits. This is a common characteristic of people from that region. A small but important detail."

Capp had to agree. Possibly even a life-preserving detail.

What Capp had volunteered to do some said was Quixotic, even suicidal. The Russians had in their custody an American espionage agent, Milo Kelly, whose cover as a correspondent had never really concealed much from anyone. The KGB had long tolerated many such "correspondents," recognizing their usefulness as conduits for false information. But now the Russians had Kelly under arrest, and there was much publicity about it in the American papers.

Shortly after the arrest had come the Russian offer: Kelly in exchange for Aleksei Korolenko, a Russian-born American scientist who had been captured four years before while attempting to defect to the east via Yugoslavia with a suitcase full of classified ICBM auto-range missile specifications. Korolenko had been tried, convicted and imprisoned, along with whatever potentially harmful data he'd memorized. The American government would have thought long and hard about such a secret exchange but for one important factor: Korolenko had died of pneumonia in federal prison two days before. So the exchange was immediately agreed upon.

Capp was to impersonate Korolenko on the east-west bridge where the exchange was to take place. There was a superficial resemblance between the two men, and it was unlikely that anyone who would be on the Soviet side of the bridge had seen Korolenko in many years if at all. But the obsessively suspicious Russians weren't fools, and everything had to sit right with them in even the smallest matter for the exchange to work.

The theory was that after the exchange the Russians would remain silent to save face. Then Capp's release could be negotiated, possibly for the return of another political prisoner valuable to the Russians, but less valuable to the Americans than was Kelly. As far as the Russians were supposed to know, Capp was merely a U.S. Army volunteer. When all the shuffling about of players on the board was over, theoretically the American side would be ahead a square.

It was another of the many extreme and dangerous plans being hatched at the time by the new regime in ACTIVE, a subbranch that would mercifully be deactivated in a few years. But during that period it seemed worth almost any risk to stay one up on the KGB in minor coups. Careers depended on it, on both sides.

"It will come to you, darling," Alanna said, kissing Capp reassuringly on the forehead, "when it has to."

"It always has," Capp said.

Their anxieties were acknowledged in a glance into each other's eyes. Each of them had come to dread the date of the exchange, now only two days away, when Capp would be flown to Bremen. Capp had never told Alanna of his doubts, of his sometimes almost overwhelming compulsion to back out of his part of the plan. Until Alanna he would never have considered such a move.

Later he realized that while he might have considered quitting, he would never have done so. They knew that much about him, and more. Possibly more than he would ever know about himself.

"It is an insane plan!" Alanna suddenly whispered fiercely yet sadly.

Capp shrugged. "In an insane world. It will work."

God help him, he believed it! Or believed he believed it!

She nodded and turned away.

Capp left her to go to a meeting with the operations coordinator, then to view fifty-five minutes of film of Korolenko taken in 1955, when the FBI had first begun to suspect him.

The operations coordinator was Dwayne Stauker.

☒ 10

THE KOROLENKO OPERATION had been attempted over twenty years ago. And the assistant director in ACTIVE who had originated the plan was Victor Wezenski—the same Victor Wezenski who went on to leave the Outfit and pursue a political, then an advertising career, and then become White House appointments secretary for President Andrew Berwin.

Wezenski was an affable, voluble man of sixty-one, with a smile-creased jowly face framed by a trimmed white beard and topped by a fringe of white hair. He favored tweedy suits and wing-tip shoes, smoked expensive greenish-black cigars in a graceful ebony holder, and all in all fit very neatly the public image of a writer.

For a writer was what Wezenski now professed to be, which was why he was present at the Crime Writers Convention at the Claremore Hotel in New York.

He'd enjoyed writing his Gateway *roman à clef, Hellgate,* and when he got back to San Francisco he intended to begin another, more ambitious novel; something really serious this time, possibly focusing on some natural disaster and perverted sex.

Wezenski sipped the scotch and soda he'd gotten at the cash bar and looked across the Claremore's Imperial Room at the many writers and mystery fans milling about and talking animatedly with each other. He was enjoying the convention and his new, slower-paced role in life. Mystery writers seemed a congenial lot, less arty and pretentious than writers in general. Though no less talented. Wezenski had always relished a good mystery and appreciated its intricacies. He considered Raymond Chandler one of the finest writers this country had produced.

Not that *Hellgate* could be compared to Chandler's work. But the novel was timely and entertaining, and Wezenski's agent, Mark Barrington, had negotiated a lucrative contract with one of New York's largest publishers. Already the book was in its third printing, and sales had not yet peaked. Even Chandler had not experienced such immediate success.

"Mr. Wezenski? Would you be so kind? . . ."

An elderly woman in a biege dress was extending a copy of *Hellgate* toward him along with a soft-tipped pen. Wezenski smiled at her, took the book and autographed it with a smooth flourish.

"I hope you enjoyed it, ma'am," he said, handing back book and pen.

"Oh, very much," the woman mumured, somewhat embarrassed. "The characters were so *real.*" She moved off into the press of people near the bar.

Wezenski remained smiling. He liked to sign autographs. He liked the company of other writers and the fans, and he liked the Imperial Room with its arched, skylighted ceiling and gilded ornate walls. The Claremore was one of New York's older hotels, with more carpeting, wood paneling and service than tile, plasterboard and mindless routine. When he returned to New York he would stay here again.

An announcement was being made at the lectern by one of the convention's directors.

"For the next half hour several of the professional writers in attendance will be in the Anderson Suite on the sixth floor to autograph copies of their books."

Wezenski glanced at his convention program and remembered that he was slated to take part in the autographing session. He hurried off toward the elevators, ahead of the many fans who'd begun to move in that direction. As he walked past the row of hotel phones, he barely noticed a large, dark-complexioned man with his back turned to him.

The man was dialing the extension number of Victor Wezenski's room to make sure no one was there.

By the time the half hour was up, Wezenski's hand ached from signing autographs. He was glad that nothing was scheduled for the next hour. Then would come a screening of the original English version of *Silver Blaze*, a vintage Sherlock Holmes film. After the film came a break for dinner, followed by a talk by the New York medical examiner, then a series of panel discussions and speeches. Wezenski had agreed to give a brief speech and answer questions on the future of the political novel. It would be a trying evening, and the next hour would be his only real chance to rest.

He stood up from the autograph table, shook a few hands, smiled a few smiles, and left to go up to the quiet of his room.

Five minutes after Wezenski had left the Anderson Suite, his agent, Mark Barrington, walked in. Barrington was a stout, graying man with a neat Vandyke beard and thick glasses with square wire frames. He glanced around and asked Graham Shore, another writer, if he had seen Victor.

"He was here," Shore said, screwing the cap on a gold pen. "He probably went back downstairs. Or maybe he's in his room."

Barrington thanked Shore and left to check. He had good news for Wezenski about an offer from Randall King, producer of socially significant movies. Wezenski had only to sign his consent to what Barrington considered to be a very advantageous contract and *Hellgate* would be made into a movie. And the 10 percent commission would make Barrington's year.

At the elevators, Barrington stood for a moment debating whether to check the Imperial Room off the lobby or to take an elevator to where Wezenski's room was located on the twelfth floor. He pressed both the up and down buttons and decided to take whichever elevator arrived first.

Wezenski turned the key in his hotel room door, pushed the door open and stepped into the short entrance hall. He was thinking, as he often had during the past three days, of how different was the crime of fiction from the crime of reality. To many people downstairs, crime was a bloodless Agatha Christie novel or an orderly police procedural progressing in a straight line toward the neat, inevitable conclusion. Wezenski supposed that was why they called it fiction. He had to admit, it was a pleasant deception.

He walked to the bed and sat down on it, bending to remove his shoes. During the past few years he'd begun to feel old, and even remotely regretful of some of the peccadilloes of his younger days. If the people downstairs only knew . . . He stretched out on his back on the bed and closed his eyes, grateful that few people did know.

Relaxation wouldn't come. Something disturbing, indefinable, was gnawing at the edges of his mind. It wouldn't go away.

He opened his eyes.

The blinds on the windows near the bed were slanted to block out the late afternoon light. Wezenski hadn't left them that way, and the maid had straightened up early that morning.

He heard a faint whisper of air, turned his head and for an instant saw the blur of bare arm, the solemn Latin face. The face was in some way familiar. The arm wielded a knife.

Wezenski's body arched on the bed as the pain drove the breath from him. It was exactly like the heart attack he'd suffered two years ago. He saw nothing but a blinding light, and his body, now painless, seemed suddenly weightless and adrift.

The brightness deepened to red, the red to black.

And deeper still . . .

Wezenski died almost instantly, without uttering the cry that bubbled to his lips.

Raul struck with the knife a few more times, in amateur

fashion, letting the blade glance off the ribs. It was a cheap hunting knife, untraceable. He dropped it beside the bed, along with the rubber gloves he'd worn.

A sudden loud knock on the door.

Raul stood very still, watching the blood from Wezenski's wounds redden the mattress in an almost symmetrical circle.

"Victor?" Three more loud knocks. "It's Mark Barrington."

Still Raul didn't move. He knew the door had locked automatically and whoever was in the hall wouldn't have a key.

Someone else might have panicked, forced the door to the connecting room, hoping to find the room empty so they could leave that way and escape. Raul was aware of the option but discarded it. There was only one man in the hall, he was sure, and if it came to a confrontation . . .

A minute passed with grudging slowness. Raul stood counting the seconds by the soft pat of blood that now dripped regularly onto the carpet.

There were no more knocks, no more sounds from the hall.

Whoever Barrington was, he must have decided Wezenski wasn't in his room.

Raul reached into his pocket and drew out a stick of bright-red lipstick he'd bought that morning at a department store cosmetic-counter. On the dresser mirror and on the walls near the bed he printed DEATH TO FASISTS, carefully misspelling *fascists* each time.

Then he replaced the lipstick in his pocket, double-checked to make sure he'd left no fingerprints and left the room.

When the elevator he'd taken down reached the lobby, half a dozen people were waiting to press in as he and two other passengers stepped out.

"I'm sure he said he was going to his room," a woman among those moving into the elevator said.

"He's not there. I checked," replied the man behind her in a voice that might have been the one in the hall outside Wezenski's door. "I need his signature on this damn thing."

Raul placidly stared straight ahead and walked across the carpeted lobby toward an exit.

At precisely ten that evening the phone at the Capp home rang twice. Capp lifted the receiver and found that no one was on the line. He knew that Raul had succeeded.

"Whoever it was, they hung up," Capp said to Myra, returning to the televised ball game he'd been watching. He was puzzled for a few moments. A home run had been hit in his absence.

☒ 11

Mark Haggar was driving home late from a chess club meeting that Monday night and at a few minutes past midnight heard the news of Victor Wezenski's murder broadcast from the car radio.

Murder.

There was no doubt of it this time.

A coldness seemed to drop along Haggar's spine and settle deep in his stomach. He pulled his Cadillac Seville to the curb and sat with both hands on the steering wheel. The motor idled soundlessly.

"Stabbed to death," the news report had said, without elaborating. The words had been loosed from the radio's speaker into the Cadillac's quiet interior with a mind-numbing suddenness. Wezenski was one of those men impossible to imagine in death.

Haggar absently turned off the radio before pulling back out into the street. As he unconsciously increased his speed, light from the overhead streetlamps rippled in smooth shadowed patterns along the Cadillac's gleaming black hood. He slowed down at an intersection with a flashing yellow light when a bearded man standing precariously balanced on the curb shouted an obscenity at him.

When he arrived home, Haggar went immediately to the phone in his study and dialed David Wellman's number.

The phone rang six times. When Wellman answered, his voice was slurred and he was obviously irritated.

"David, this is Mark," Haggar said brusquely.

Wellman made an unsuccessful attempt to come completely awake. "Mark, this is pretty damn late to be calling." His voice was still thick, dragging like a slowly played record.

"I just heard on the news that Victor Wezenski's been murdered."

At least ten seconds passed before Wellman replied in a calm, clear voice, "Where, when, why and by whom?"

"They don't know who did it or why. The where and when is in his New York hotel room sometime today. Or yesterday," Haggar amended, glancing at his watch. "He was stabbed to death."

"What was he doing in New York?"

Haggar was impressed by Wellman's composure, his business-as-usual tone.

"He was at some kind of mystery writers convention," Haggar said. "He was supposed to give a speech and plug his book."

"His book should sell well now."

"That might be the least important of his murder's ramifications."

"Drake and then eight days later Wezenski," Wellman replied. "I admit it seems like more than coincidence. But still it might be. I'd feel worse about it if Wezenski had died in an accident. People get murdered in New York every day."

"Not former White House staff members," Haggar said.

"Any apparent motive? Was he robbed?"

"The news report didn't elaborate." Haggar picked up his meerschaum pipe from the rack on his desk, tapped it a few times on his knee, then held it unlighted in his left hand. "We can't discount the possibility that it has something to do with Lazarus," he said cautiously.

"I suppose not. We can't afford to discount anything, or to leap to any conclusions without sufficient facts. We'll be able to learn more about Wezenski's death later this morning."

Haggar could not contain the nervousness in his voice as he said, "Under any circumstances the two deaths so close together just can't be ignored. If it's a coincidence, it's the sort of coincidence we've been trained not to believe in. I think one of us should talk to Whitencroft."

"Maybe. Go ahead and call him tomorrow. When we know more about Wezenski. Let me know what he said."

After Haggar hung up, he packed the meerschaum with tobacco from his suede pocket pouch. It was oddly comforting to know that Wellman was somewhat alarmed. At least it meant that Hagar wasn't necessarily the anxiety-ridden recluse he sometimes felt himself becoming.

When the pipe was fired up, Haggar walked from his study and sat in the overstuffed chair near the living room bookcases. He knew there was no way for him to sleep; the coldness still lay like a slab of ice in his stomach, causing a dull ache now that made him want to hunch his shoulders. He refused to recognize it as fear.

He stood up and walked to the liquor cabinet to pour himself some cognac. The bottle was empty. That damned Nora; he'd always suspected her of sneaking an occasional nip from the cabinet. Or had he finished the cognac a few nights ago? He replaced the empty bottle so violently that it might have cracked, but he didn't bother examining it before closing the cherrywood doors.

There was a lounge in the next block where Haggar had once stopped for a few drinks. Larry's Rest Stop was its name, a respectable and discreet place of soft music and angled, private upholstered booths. Not a place of fear and loneliness. There would be people there, talking quietly and laughing, and a friendly nod from the bartender and a snifter of warming Courvoisier.

When Haggar walked to the door he found that he didn't want to go out. His stomach fluttered and he saw that his fingers were trembling.

Shaking off that unreasonable hesitation with a self-deprecating grin, he stepped out into the hall and locked the door carefully behind him.

At Larry's, Haggar noticed that he was the only one drinking alone. And the Courvoisier did little to assuage the cold ache deep within him. Within fifteen minutes he left to return home.

The night seemed darker and emptier than usual.

Haggar walked wishing that morning would hurry so he could phone Whitencroft.

☒ 12

THE MORNING CALL of an owl outside the Capps' two-story house awoke Capp, and he lay curled on his side in bed beside Myra and listened as the owl called three more times in quick succession. He didn't mind the regular morning rudeness of the owl. It was much preferable to the annoying cooing of pigeons in the eaves outside the window, which is what he'd had to endure until the owl had recently moved into the big walnut tree in the side yard. Where there were owls, other birds seldom ventured.

The drapes were pulled shut and the bedroom was still dim and restful. Opposite the bed was an antique vanity cluttered with Myra's cosmetics and a brush-and-comb set. A large Victorian wardrobe that served as Capp's closet towered against another wall, its scrolled top casting rounded cloud-like shadows about its crown. The pale-yellow walls were adorned with gilt-framed landscapes, neutral and soothing like the rest of the room.

Myra was awake beside Capp. They lay silently for a while, each unwilling to acknowledge their wakefulness. Then they talked aimlessly for a few minutes and decided to have breakfast out.

Capp rose and switched on the TV near the foot of the bed. It was his and Myra's custom to look in on the morning network news as they dressed.

He was standing in stockinged feet and choosing a shirt from the Victorian wardrobe when the newscaster announced Wezenski's murder. Moving back to the bed, Capp sat on the edge of the mattress and bent to slip on his shoes as he watched the TV screen.

The newscaster described without emotion how Wezenski had been found stabbed to death in his hotel room, and how the words *death to fascists* had been found crudely scrawled on the walls in lipstick. The police had no suspect as yet, but the killer had left behind the murder weapon and a pair of rubber gloves that might provide a lead.

No mention was made of the word *fascists* being misspelled; that was something the police were keeping to themselves. And much was made of the irony of Wezenski being murdered in a hotel filled with some of the country's top thriller writers. A few of the writers were interviewed. One of them, a short, Italian-looking man, was in an obviously excited state and advanced the theory that the killer had gained access to Wezenski's room by lowering himself on a rope from the window of the vacant room above.

Capp watched blankly as he tied his left shoe. The site of Wezenski's death had been well chosen; the police would soon be deluged with bizarre as well as very reasonable theories as to how, why and by whom the crime was committed. And procedure-prone types that they were, the police would be rendered impotent in a sea of plausible possibilities advanced by avid crime aficionados, none of which were correct. The more possibilities, the more work involved. Until time cooled all leads.

A wise choice, too, to let it be known that Wezenski was murdered. Capp knew that made it all the more unlikely that the newly affluent author's death would be linked to Drake's.

Myra was also watching the TV, seated on her small vanity bench, which she'd moved over by the window. She was wearing blue slacks and a bra, the flesh of her stomach lapping over the elastic waistband of the slacks as she strained forward in concentration.

The news cut to an interview with an Arab leader in a tailored blue business suit.

"Don't expect me to say I'm sorry," Capp said. "Wezenski was a bastard all the way down the line."

Myra nodded, stood and slipped a blouse over her head, being careful not to disarrange her hair.

Capp tied his right shoe, quietly basking in the success of Wezenski's execution.

From the kitchen below came the scent of fresh-brewed coffee. Capp looked at the clock by the bed. The automatic coffee maker had begun its work a few minutes before. When the coffee was ready, the timer would switch the burner to warm and keep coffee available most of the day. Capp had bought the coffee maker the week before; he had a fondness for gadgetry.

He sniffed the air in exaggerated fashion. "Do you want a cup before we leave?"

Myra shook her head no and stepped into stub-toed shoes with high, laminated-wood heels. She checked her hair carefully in the vanity mirror and made some last-minute adjustments with her comb.

In the car on the way to the restaurant she was silent, and throughout breakfast she said very little.

But by the time they arrived back home, she was herself again.

☒ 13

ANDREW BERWIN HAD FINISHED breakfast by ten o'clock and was alone in his office awaiting the scheduled telephone call from Whitencroft. The white phone from the wall cabinet was before him on the desk, and he sat glaring at it morosely as if expecting it to defy him in some manner. From outside came the muted, nasal moan of a power mower. Overseen by the Secret Service, the local landscaping company that had contracted to keep the lawn trimmed was hard at work.

A few seconds after the sweep-second hand of the brass wall clock passed twelve, the light on the phone began to blink. The phone made no sound.

Berwin lifted the receiver and pressed it to his ear. He waited patiently for the voice on the other end of the line.

"Hello? . . ."

"Hello, Alex."

"You've heard the news, I suppose," Whitencroft said.

"About Wezenski? Yes. Tragedy there." Berwin settled back into his oversized desk chair that made him appear curiously deflated. He'd genuinely liked Wezenski. The man's ebullient spirit, though at times a liability, was one of the few bright memories of the second, abbreviated term. Berwin began tapping a gold pen rhythmically on his kneecap. "Have the polls indicated any shift in California?"

"There are no recent polls of any significance."

"Ah, perhaps that in itself is significant. I want you to continue close liaison, keep the string taut."

"No problem there."

"That's nice to hear," Berwin said almost wistfully. "We're not used to sailing calm seas. But we can't be lulled into making false assumptions."

"No, sir."

Berwin waited. By the tone of Whitencroft's voice, he obviously had something more on his mind.

The voice came over the line as if squeezed through by a vague uneasiness. "Mark Haggar phoned me earlier this morning. In fact, very early this morning."

"About Wezenski, no doubt."

"Yes," Whitencroft said. "Haggar and Wellman talked last night after Haggar caught the news on his car radio. They're concerned, especially Haggar. They think there might be some connection between the deaths of Drake and Wezenski."

"That same thought had occurred to me," Berwin said, "but there's nothing really to lend credence to the idea."

"No, there's no similarity whatsoever in the way they died. I suppose one might view that in itself as possibly suspicious."

"You have the background to understand these things. Are you suspicious?"

Whitencroft hesitated only an instant. " 'Suspicious' is too strong a word. Yet I don't feel we can completely disregard the coincidence of the two unnatural deaths occurring within weeks of each other. We should keep an eye on the Wezenski investigation. I contacted someone I know in the New York Police Department, inquiring in the role of a friend of Wezenski."

"What do the police think at this point?"

"They think nothing. They're confronted with dozens of possibilities: a burglar who was interrupted, a political killing, a grudge murder, a professional killer, an amateur . . . Unless someone talks, it's one of those crimes that probably will never be solved."

"Surely there are clues of some sort," Berwin said.

"Too many clues, too many theories, none of them substantial."

Berwin noticed that Whitencroft pronounced it "substa-shual." Whitencroft always sounded as if he had a cold when talking on the other end of a phone call.

"All we can do then is watch the situation," Berwin said, wondering what exactly Whitencroft expected of him.

"Haggar and Wellman need some sort of reassurance concerning their safety."

"What do they expect, bodyguards?"

"They didn't specify. But that seems a bit premature."

Berwin was suddenly aggravated. "Then tell them I said they were safe," he snapped.

Whitencroft let the subject drop. "I'll stay on top of things out west. Any messages to convey there?"

"I think not at this point. Keep me apprised of what's going on. Your next scheduled phone call is at the regular time, morning after next."

"Yes, sir."

"And Alex," Berwin added before hanging up, "tell Haggar, Wellman and the others that I'm doing everything possible to ensure their safety."

"I will, sir."

When Berwin had replaced the phone in its hidden recess, he began to pace about his office with his upper body bent forward, hands clasped behind his back. He was aware that he cut a dramatically Napoleonic figure and would not have carried himself that way if others were present. But he was alone, so he could hardly be accused of being theatrical. Pacing in such a manner was entirely natural to him even if others wouldn't understand. It helped him to think.

He stopped pacing and sat on the edge of his desk with his arms folded loosely in front of him, settling into an easy, informal pose. He licked his lips.

The large things were under control; yet he felt some of the small and relatively insignificant matters slipping from his grasp. It had often been that way in the past, and the seemingly insignificant, once free of his control, occasionally had taken on a new significance and danger.

At times Berwin felt like a fighting bull being baited in the ring, stronger by far than any single opponent yet infuriated and weakened by a hundred small agonies.

Helen's behavior was becoming a constant if tiny tormenting thorn in his existence. She was visiting their daughter Sandra in Vermont. Berwin didn't so much mind Helen's believing she was roaming the country without his knowing her whereabouts, but he *was* stung by the fact that Sandra hadn't phoned him. Was his wife poisoning his eldest daughter's mind against her own father? Sandra had always been Berwin's favorite, though he'd never admitted that to anyone, including Helen. But Helen knew. In that accommodating, saccharine way of hers, she had always sensed his vulnerabilities. The layers of knowledge the years gave a wife! . . .

Berwin straightened and walked around behind the wide desk. He drew a small gold ring of keys from his pocket and opened a bottom drawer. From the drawer he got a bottle of port and a glass. Though it was still early, he poured himself a small drink.

Berwin drank only port now, and that very seldom. And he made it a point to keep any liquor and its accounterments from everyone's view. He remembered the vicious rumor and innuendo that had accompanied his final days in office. Oh, within some of it lay small kernels of truth, but Berwin had learned how the truth could be turned against even the best of men. There were those who used truth only as a foundation to support their malicious exaggerations and horrendous distortions.

He drank the port more quickly than he had planned and replaced glass and bottle in the deep drawer, locking it carefully.

Then Berwin sat down at his desk and opened a legal-size yellow file folder and began studying its contents. The folder contained questions that were to be asked in a second series of televised taped interviews to which he'd agreed. Few but the very wise would believe his answers, he was sure, but still it was worth the effort to attempt again to set the record straight. His memoirs and infrequent public appearances hadn't accomplished that.

He sat hunched square-shouldered over the desk, breathing deeply and evenly as he read. His answers must be phrased with the utmost care; the vultures of the media still circled over what they thought to be his political carcass. Well, they had done that before and been surprised.

But Berwin found himself having difficulty concentrating. The neatly typed words before him would swim and lose meaning and his eyes would stray to focus on nothing.

He wondered what he actually could do to protect Haggar and Wellman. It was imperative that nothing should happen to them, though in all probability they were in no danger. The situation now was one of only nagging concern, yet Berwin sensed within it the potential for catastrophe.

The high drone of the power mower outside seemed louder, probing like a thin wire into Berwin's agitated brain.

He pressed an intercom button with a sudden, almost spastic motion.

"God damn them," he said, "can't they cut grass farther from the house? Or use electric mowers?"

He switched off the intercom so he wouldn't be aggravated by the banal, subservient reply.

Within less than a minute the drone of the mower ceased. Berwin realized regretfully that his outburst was unworthy of him, certainly uncharacteristic.

He reached again for the drawer that contained the bottle. His fingers trembled.

Remembering the sound of the old reel-type push mowers, he almost smiled. Now there was a sound that relaxed, the rhythmic clicking of metal on metal as the mower was pushed to arm's length, then the higher, ratchety sound as it was pulled back. It was the sound of a man doing a job without an engine performing most of the work.

Long ago, when he and Helen had first moved to Washington, when they were young and their daughters were children, Berwin used to cut the grass in front of their small frame house every weekend, hoping some enterprising photographer from one of the papers would think to get a shot of him at work like any other homeowner, any other voter. And sure enough, finally it had happened. The photo had appeared in the *Post*, with a nice accompanying story and quotes from Helen and the girls.

Berwin felt a tightening sensation at the back of his throat and swallowed. So much about the past was preferable to the present.

He looked down and saw that his fingers were now steady.

Without removing the bottle, he closed his desk drawer.

Neither the past nor the present was preferable, he told himself. It was all in the way a person looked at things, and in what was intended for the future.

☒ 14

THE DRONE OF A distant power mower sounded faintly through the Oberammergau training facilities. The monotonous sustained note of the small gasoline engine soothed Dwayne Stauker, made the complexities of his position seem somehow manageable.

In 1960 Stauker's thick gray hair had been even thicker, attempting to stand out from his head in unruly ringlets though he combed it straight back, and it was so black as to have a bluish tint to it. He ran an exploring hand delicately a quarter inch beyond the perimeter of his dark hair to make sure it was in place, and he stared at Capp with small but alert gray eyes, the sort of eyes sometimes described as shooter's eyes.

Capp instinctively disliked Stauker. But then they hadn't just been made fraternity roommates. It was quite possible that after today he would never see Stauker again.

The Sikorsky helicopter was to arrive this afternoon to transport Capp to Bremen, then east to Hamburg near where the exchange was to take place.

"It will only be necessary to fool the Russian party for some twenty minutes," Stauker said evenly, "so remember, for those twenty minutes you are to *be* Aleksei Korolenko."

"I'm more Korolenko than I am myself," Capp replied. He was standing with his weight evenly distributed on the balls of his feet, disdaining to lean against the nearby table or wall. Russians generally didn't lean. It was to amaze Capp some years later that such shallow subterfuge had lent him such deep confidence.

The room they were in might have been the sitting room of an ordinary middle-class merchant. A sculpted maroon rug was perfectly centered, framed by waxed and gleaming hardwood. There were a small gray brocaded sofa, a piecrust table supporting a vase of artificial chrysanthemums, and a brick fireplace the cavity of which was covered by an elegant triangular fan braced between polished brass andirons. On a bookcase cluttered with glass curios was a series of family photos, formidable-looking women and dark, dour men with mustaches. Capp knew the room was an exact replica of a genuine lived-in room, possibly hundreds or even thousands of miles away.

Capp watched as Stauker paced to the window and fingered the artificial chrysanthemums. Stauker emanated a certain smoothness that suggested calm confidence and was at the same time somehow intimidating. He saw himself as a genuine piss-cutter with a future. And how he did like to play the role.

"You don't need to be reminded of how much is riding on this," he said to Capp, still examining the chrysanthemums as if they were real and afflicted with some curious plant disease.

"No," Capp said, "I don't need to be reminded."

Stauker turned and gave him an odd glance. "You'll once more go through the detailed presentation of Korolenko's life, and it's the seeming trivialities that will bear the greatest danger. The Russians might have a few trick questions to quickly affirm identity and condition of mental faculties. They've used that method before."

Capp held his hands before him spread palms down, a Korolenko gesture that was now second nature. "We can prepare for that only on the basis of what we know, but I think I'm ready to handle whatever they throw our way."

"If it can be handled."

"If not, we whiff."

"And the short- and long-range consequences of that might be damned unpleasant for all concerned."

Capp knew which of the concerned Stauker was thinking most about.

"We're to meet at the exact center of the bridge at twenty-two hundred sharp," Stauker said. "We'll—"

He was interrupted by three evenly spaced knocks on the door.

Stauker went to open the door and Capp almost expected to see the room's inhabitant, perhaps an elderly, puzzled woman laden with grocery bags, standing wearily, wondering who'd invaded her home. But it was Tripp who'd knocked.

Tripp was a silent, bull-necked German attached to Control in some undisclosed fashion. His wide trap mouth was arched downward and his angled brows set in a frown as he beckoned Stauker out into the hall. Capp heard whispers, then the sound of both men walking hurriedly away.

A full fifteen minutes passed before Stauker returned alone. He looked down at Capp, who was sitting on the small gray sofa. Stauker pulled the corners of his mouth down with a wiping motion of thumb and forefinger. Much of the color had left his face and his dark hair was mussed on the right side where he'd run his hand through it.

"It's off," he said.

Capp stood, not understanding. "Off? . . . Meaning what? . . ."

Stauker looked hopelessly at him, as if whatever had gone wrong could be laid to Capp. "The Russians called off the exchange. They became suspicious. Control learned just half an hour ago." He slammed a fist into his open palm and snorted angrily.

Then Stauker's tension seemed to leave him and only disappointment remained to cloud the narrow gray eyes. "The Russians sent Control a series of seemingly simple questions about Korolenko—the sort of questions you'd expect them to ask: his weight, the state of his health, his mental alertness

. . . Most of the medical questions concerned Korolenko's congenital heart condition, which in part was the cause of his death. But the bastards also slipped in something about gallstones that threw Control. It seems that Korolenko had had his gall bladder removed, and he had never informed us. Maybe he forgot the operation; maybe he thought it would be useful in the future if he concealed the information. But apparently the Russians came up with that fact on his medical record, and it was something we didn't know about and tripped over."

"Maybe they can be reassured."

"It's too late; it's scrubbed. It's a whiff."

Capp sat back down. He wasn't sure how he felt. Relief? Yes, he had to admit relief. He wondered if he'd have felt this much relief if it weren't for Alanna. His heart was racing and his fingertips were cold and on the verge of trembling. It was almost as if the mission were still on and he was about to begin the walk onto the wide bridge over the Elbe. He'd thought so much about that hypothetical moment, moved through it in his training and in his sleep. After thoroughly exploring his fear, he'd assumed he could cope with it.

Capp sat with his elbows on his knees, his head bowed. He knew he should say something, but just then all he could think about was Alanna. Alanna and what he'd almost lost. For he could admit to himself now that the odds on his return were even at best.

Yet, perhaps influenced by Stauker, he couldn't escape the feeling that in some way the operation's failure was his fault, that somehow he'd let everyone down.

When he looked up, Stauker was gone, and Capp was alone in the warm and homey room. Someone else's room.

"I'm to go to Bonn," Capp said that night to Alanna.

Alanna sipped her cognac, stared into it and swirled the brandy as if prompting it for answers. "That's not so far," she said. She was wearing only a man's long flannel plaid shirt that came almost to her knees. It seemed incredible that she could find a shirt that size. "We can see each other. If that's what you want."

Capp was seated in a wicker chair opposite her, mesmerized by the fluidity of her pale and lissome body. Each of her movements seemed to leave a graceful tracing in the air.

"There's nothing I'll ever want more," he said.

Alanna tossed down the rest of her cognac, a feat she was able to accomplish delicately. It often amazed Capp how much she could drink, seemingly without effect.

He sipped his own drink and watched the long-stemmed girl replenish her long-stemmed glass. Really he knew little about her, and she about him. And what they did know about each other embodied only the present. Players in a game of life and death, theirs was a world of tenuous friends and cautious lovers.

At the end of the week, Capp left for Bonn and months of desk work and courier duty.

He enjoyed Bonn. It was a small city of baroque but appealing architecture and an undercurrent of intrigue and officialdom everywhere. It was, other than Berlin, where the action was in Germany.

Often Alanna would drive up and spend days at a time with him. Capp thought the situation would be nearly ideal if by some chance she could be assigned duty in Bonn.

And Alanna was reassigned. But not to Bonn, to Beirut. She withheld the information until the night before her departure to Lebanon. Their farewell over dinner at the American Club was tearless and all the sadder for being so. The French had an expression that described such a situation, but it escaped Capp's memory and he decided piss on the French.

Capp was determined that the affair not end. In his daily existence of shifting values and perspectives, the one thing he knew was that he loved Alanna, that he missed her. He wrote. She didn't answer. It was Alanna who was the realist of the two.

Two months after her departure Capp heard she had married Dwayne Stauker.

The Outfit understood when a man was on the edge; they didn't like it. Capp was shuffled to London and placed on leave to sort himself out.

Most of the time he spent in his rented room, or walking the streets near where he lived off Chattington Square. Twice during the week after his arrival he had lain in bed with the gas hissing flamelessly from the room's coin-operated space heater, but both times he had risen and twisted the valve to off. He wasn't sure himself if he'd actually intended going through with suicide; he knew, objectively, that he was acting the fool. But he wasn't being objective. He couldn't be.

Then one day it no longer mattered. Not on a conscious level. Capp would always love Alanna, but finally he'd been able to compartmentalize his emotions. What he couldn't kill, he buried alive. And he set about doing what he knew he had to do, molding an impenetrable protective shell about himself. On a day-to-day basis, it no longer mattered. Except for that precarious moment before waking.

He returned to work.

And during the following years he even learned to be civil to Stauker. It was a source of secret pride to Capp that he and Stauker worked more effectively now as a team than they had before Stauker's marriage to Alanna.

Then, in Virginia, Capp had met Myra Edelman, an operations clerk on a minor security level. She was a shapely, innately cheerful woman with a quick, too-friendly smile and fanciful clear blue eyes. Rumor had it that a man named Callaway, a reader in Assimilation, had gotten her pregnant and talked her into an abortion, then deserted her. She handled that rumor with admirable aplomb.

But Capp could see that she hated Callaway. In his presence, a rage and shame seemed to run like a violet current through her clear eyes; but she said nothing.

Capp discreetly investigated and found that the rumors

were true. Admiration mixed with pity is the genesis of love. Capp began seeing Myra Edelman regularly.

Six months later they were married. Dwayne and Alanna Stauker attended the wedding.

Capp had thought that his wedding was also an exorcism to free him of Alanna. He'd thought that for years. Until her mangled body had been found in a mad metal sculpture alongside a flat Texas highway.

Then, in his memory, she had stirred.

☒ 15

STANDING AT HIS OFFICE window, Berwin watched the royal blue Lincoln limousine clear security at the gate and glide down the road to pass beyond his view. He half expected to see Helen in the rear of the car, but only the Secret Service driver was visible. The lower sides of the long car were splattered with mud from the recent rain. Berwin made a mental note of the mud and would find out this afternoon why the car hadn't been washed.

The Lincoln was a 1979 model, and Berwin wondered how many like it had been manufactured. How closely had the guard at the gate looked at the driver, checked the license plate?

It was possible that Mark Haggar's apprehension was justified. Perhaps there was a link between the deaths of Charles Drake and Victor Wezenski. If so, it was possible that there would be future links in a chain of deaths.

Berwin sat at his desk and punched a telephone button. He summoned Art Rapaport, the Secret Service security chief at Lost Palms, to his office.

Rapaport knocked on the door within a minute and was admitted. He was a tall, slender man with straight blond hair thinning at the crown, quick pink-rimmed eyes and long, jut-jawed Scandinavian features that conveyed an impression of sad alertness and intelligence. His face was slightly mottled but smooth, as if he'd just shaved. He was wearing that sort of brown-black anonymous suit favored by his breed, a loosely knotted blue-striped tie and black dress boots. The left lapel of his suit coat was inverted at the side of his neck; he'd hurriedly slipped the coat on out of deference to Berwin. Berwin motioned with a short, crisp movement of his arm and Rapaport sat down in one of the small but comfortable chairs near the desk.

Berwin sat with his hands before him on the desk top, his fingertips extended to within a hairbreadth of the corresponding fingertips on the opposite hand. He was staring at his hands as if he expected that at any moment an electrical current would arc between his fingertips.

"I think perhaps security measures should be tightened," he said.

"I can increase them, sir."

"Oh, I don't think we're at that point, Art." Berwin folded his hands convulsively as if some magnetic force had been suddenly reversed. "I don't want measures so much increased as intensified. You understand, have the guards be more alert. There are natural slacking-off periods . . ."

As Berwin spoke he was gazing out the tall window. There had been no need to install bulletproof glass in the frame, as the window looked out over flat lawn, sand and the narrow road from the inner gate. Then the land fell away gradually to a high fence. There simply was no place a gunman could find cover outside the window even if he did manage to penetrate the Lost Palms defenses to that point. But for a moment Berwin considered ordering the special glass installed. Then he remembered that he had the office window open much of the time anyway. The stale, chemical-tainted chill of air conditioning sometimes depressed him.

"Is it the Drake-Wezenski thing, sir?" Rapaport asked.

"Well, I suppose we should take those incidents into consideration. As part of an overall tightening up process."

Significant, Berwin thought, that Rapaport had said "Drake-Wezenski," that he should link the two deaths in mind and speech. Those in his business developed uncanny intuition.

Rapaport nodded his narrow head and sat calmly, hunched slightly forward in his chair in the seemingly disjointed manner of tall men. "I'll talk to all personnel," he said, "and run a series of inspections myself on those assigned to sensitive areas. Also, I can increase the frequency of remote checks on the electronic surveillance equipment."

"Yes, those are the kinds of things I had in mind. With all the political activity of late and its dominance in the news, we don't know what's going to crawl out of the woodwork, do we?"

"Whatever it is, I believe we can be ready for it, sir."

"Oh, I don't mean to impugn your performance to date. You're doing a fine job, Art, a fine job. It's just that there are times when increased alertness seems desirable."

"It can be accomplished," Rapaport said. "There's never a time when improvement is impossible."

Berwin sat back and bobbed his head slightly in agreement. He liked to hear Rapaport talk in that manner, and occasionally he wondered if the lanky Secret Service man did it to play up to him. Not that it mattered. Ambition and sound personal tactics were things he liked to see in any man. He let his body slip forward.

"Tomorrow afternoon a man is coming to see me," he said. "His name is Walter Chereno and he'll be driving a pale-blue 1975 Dodge sedan. This is the license number." Berwin handed Rapaport a folded slip of paper. "When he arrives, let him past the gates and direct him here."

Rapaport said that he would and put the slip of paper in an inside pocket of his dark suit coat.

Berwin stood up to signal Rapaport that it was time to leave. "Let me know what steps you've taken, Art."

"Yes, sir. I'll be on it immediately." Rapaport stood and moved in his lanky, shambling gait toward the door, then before leaving he turned. "If there's any reason in the future for you even to suspect that something might be tried, it will help if you let me know as soon as possible."

"Certainly," Berwin said, and remained standing after Rapaport had gone.

* * *

Walter Chereno arrived exactly on time the next afternoon.

Berwin knew when Cherano had entered the outer door, and he purposely withheld assistance in negotiating the angled maze to his office. Chereno knocked on the office door with amazingly little delay.

Berwin ushered him into the office and shook hands with him.

Chereno was a medium-height muscular man with large, capable hands and a flat stomach. His squarish face was a tanned arrangement of planes and angles accentuated by fine but deep seams on his forehead and about his eyes and the corners of his mouth. Some of the seams were scars. He had deep-set, curiously jovial black eyes behind dark-rimmed glasses, and Berwin had never seen him awed by anyone.

"You're looking well, sir," Chereno said, and he smiled and sat down. He waited while Berwin moved behind the desk and sat in the leather-upholstered swivel chair.

On one corner of the desk were an ice bucket, some glasses and a carafe of water. Berwin poured water over three ice cubes in a wide glass and handed the drink across the desk. He poured nothing for himself.

Chereno thanked Berwin and stared calmly and motionlessly at him with a faintly amused curiosity in his dark eyes. The glass of water rested unsampled and casually balanced in his tanned and weathered right hand. He was one of those men destined to appear the same at sixty as at forty. Berwin knew that he was forty-six.

Outside the window a gull screamed in what sounded like human desperation.

Yesterday Chereno had been in Topeka, Kansas. Today he was in Florida within earshot of the ocean and a deposed President.

He was about to discover why.

☒ 16

"ANOTHER BUSINESS TRIP," Capp said to Myra. "I'll be leaving tomorrow."

Myra was reading *Cosmopolitan* magazine. She nodded and continued flipping pages as she idly scanned the slick, brightly colored advertisements that promised so much.

"It's late," Capp said. "Coming to bed?"

"Soon." Myra didn't glance up.

Capp had started to rise, but he settled back down into his chair. "I'll be leaving around noon."

"All right." A page crackled as she turned it. "We could use some new furniture here and there," Myra said. "Some of what we have didn't store well."

"We can afford that," Capp said.

"How long will you be gone?"

"Probably about a week. What sort of furniture did you have in mind?"

"For the bedroom, mainly. I can watch for a sale."

"I'll return as soon as possible," Capp said. "You know that."

Myra closed the magazine and dropped it into a wooden rack alongside her chair. "I know you will."

Capp propped up his stockinged feet again on the hassock and looked up at the ceiling.

"The drawers stick," Myra said.

"What?"

"The drawers in the bedroom furniture. They've warped.

It's from having the heat off for so long in that room. Nothing seems to work right. Haven't you noticed, Will?"

"Yes. I'll pack in the morning. I won't need to take much."

"Do you want me to drive you to the airport?" Myra asked.

"No, I'll take a cab."

Myra picked up the magazine again and began leafing through it. Capp stood and went up to bed.

He lay in bed alone and wondered at his and Myra's increasing inability to communicate around the necessary secretiveness of his occupation. Or what had been his occupation and had become his way of life. Through the years they had developed a structured, circumventing code that now seemed to be failing them. The things unsaid hadn't been allowed to interfere with the workings of their daily life together. Now there seemed to be shades of deeply buried resentment in all their conversations. What was he doing to her?

The only noises in the bedroom were the faint creaking, humming sounds of the large house. They were noises that reminded Capp of the many empty houses he'd been in through the years.

He was asleep before Myra came to bed.

The next afternoon he did have her drive him to the airport, where under an alias he took a flight to Nashville, Tennessee.

From the airport in Nashville, he drove a rented car out to Route 65 and found a motel that suited him. It was the Sack Out Inn, a rambling, slightly run-down arrangement of stone duplex cabins. Not an expensive motel, but the kind that did a brisk business because it was surrounded by the newer, plusher chain motels that charged higher rates.

Capp steered into the graveled lot and parked his rented compact near the cabin with the red neon OFFICE sign in a window. Though there was plenty of daylight left, the sign was glowing, as was the large multicolored neon sign near the highway, depicting a man blissfully dozing in a sleeping bag.

Capp adjusted his clear wire-framed glasses, got out of the car and walked to the office door.

The office was paneled with knotty pine, with a red vinyl sofa and a coffee table along one wall. A faint scent of mothballs hung in the air.

Behind a long desk cluttered with country-music advertisements stood a teen-aged girl chewing gum as she tapped a pencil on the desk top in rhythm to the frantic music blasting from the radio. It was a marvel of coordination.

The girl saw Capp and turned to lower the volume. "Help you?" She tucked the pencil behind her ear, where it was nearly lost in the dark tangle of her hair.

"A single," Capp said. "Just for the night."

She continued to chew as she turned the registration tablet toward him. Capp picked up one of several cheap ball-point pens lying on the desk and signed his alias.

He paid in advance in cash and the girl gave him a key attached to a large red plastic tag in the shape of the sleeping-bag sign near the highway. "Thirty-four," the girl said, and the tag confirmed it.

As Capp began walking to where his car was parked, he heard the beat of the driving rock music swell to new heights. The crunch of his soles on the gravel seemed an odd, slow musical counterpoint.

After looking over the sterile orderliness of cabin 34, Capp walked down the highway to a truck-stop cafeteria and had the roast beef special for supper. Then he sat for a long time sipping black coffee and listening to the chatter of the truckers around him. On his way out of the cafeteria, he bought a Nashville paper to take with him back to the motel.

Capp lay on his back on the bed, propped up his head on the wadded pillow and read the paper for the next half hour. Then he stripped to his underwear, did a hundred sit-ups, three sets of twenty push-ups and twenty deep knee bends. He was breathing heavily when he had finished, and his knees demonstrated a disturbing pliancy when he walked.

Capp took a shower, then lay down again on the bed and eventually fell asleep watching an ecologically concerned girl singer on the *Tonight Show*.

The urgent buzz of the travel alarm clock on the table by the bed woke him at seven the next morning.

He rolled to sit up on the edge of the mattress and waited a few seconds while the grogginess left him. Then he took from his suitcase a flat leather case about the size of a paperback novel. Weaving slightly, he carried the case into the bathroom, along with his shaving kit and comb.

After shaving, Capp opened the leather case and went about his deft art of altering his appearance. He combed his hair again low over his forehead in uncharacteristic fashion; beneath his eyes he created a touch of shadow; and the natural lines of his face he subtly darkened and deepened. More than anything, he had aged himself.

Capp disdained such extreme disguise paraphernalia as false beards or mustaches; they never appeared quite natural to the trained eye, and there was always the possibility of them slipping partly off. Capp simply altered his appearance so that likeness became mere resemblance, and a resemblance one would have to look at twice to perceive.

He placed his wire-framed nonprescription spectacles carefully on the bridge of his nose and was satisfied. The shape of the glass frames was formulated to alter the line of his nose and cheekbones. It often amazed Capp how the appearance of the human face could be changed by the simple alteration of a few key lines or planes, and he possessed a plastic surgeon's skill at determining these key facial characteristics.

Capp double-checked the motel cabin to make sure he was leaving nothing behind, then he latched his suitcase and carried it out to his car. The morning was damp and gray, with a low sun that seemed to glower over the eastern horizon. Capp would drive for a while before stopping for breakfast.

He locked the suitcase in the car's trunk, then got in behind the steering wheel. The six-cylinder engine racketed to a start on the second twist of the ignition key.

The car's tires crunched loudly on wet gravel as Capp drove from the lot, made a right turn onto the mist-darkened highway and headed for the Kentucky state line.

Soon, on either side of the road, dense green woods stretched to angled, jagged skylines. This was hunting country, and Capp was on the hunt.

☒ 17

MARK HAGGAR HAD ARRIVED the previous day at his cabin in the low wooded hills south of Lexington, Kentucky. He had owned the cabin for years, coming to it only occasionally, when he felt the most pressing need for seclusion.

The cabin was small, but its interior belied its crude exterior of cedar-plank construction and wood roof shingles. The kitchen was a green tiled affair of modern stainless-steel gadgetry and overhead oak cabinets. On one wall was a small electric range, and on a shelf beside it was a gleaming microwave oven outfitted with an array of dials and switches. Above the sink a curtained window looked out over the winding dirt lane that led to the cabin. The lane appeared like a sweeping, irregular question mark.

In the center of the cabin was a gas-operated free-standing fireplace. The fireplace was conical and of red-enameled steel, tapering to a straight flue pipe that extended up through the roof.

Grouped around this central source of warmth were a cluster of comfortable stuffed chairs and a small crushed-velvet sofa. Wall shelves were lined with well-read books and various mementos of fishing and hunting expeditions. There was a small Formica-topped bar in the corner near the door to the kitchen. Steep stairs led up to a loft that was just large enough to accommodate a small antique chest of drawers and two double beds.

Haggar had slept late and untroubled that morning, then had a leisurely breakfast of powdered egg substitute, orange juice and aromatic herbal tea. He intended to get in his regular jogging while secluded at the cabin, combining his self-imposed sabbatical with a weight-reducing regimen.

There was no need to face up to something when it wasn't necessary, he assured himself over a second cup of tea. The decision to come to the cabin was a sound one.

Outside, a squirrel scurried among thick leaves and a jay began a strident chatter near the front window. Haggar decided to sit in one of the deck chairs on the wood front porch.

The morning had begun with clouds and a fine mist, but now the sun shone brightly through the canopy of leaves to cast dappled patterns of shadow and light over the scenic view down the lane. Haggar's dusty black Cadillac was parked to the side of the porch. As he sat down with his tea he saw what might have been raccoon tracks on the hood. Even those marks didn't disturb him, so tranquil was the setting in which he'd let himself become absorbed. A stay in the cabin seldom failed to work its tension-draining magic on him. He had brought a woman here once, long ago. Perhaps he should do so again. A man became old soon enough.

Haggar leaned back, set his mug of tea on the wide arm of the chair and propped up his feet on the porch rail. The deaths of Drake and Wezenski, the frustrating conversations with Whitencroft and Wellman, the cloying apprehension that woke him at odd hours—all of it now seemed far removed. What connection had any of it with that towering stand of cedars among the maple and oak trees? That jagged green sweep of hill to the west? The scent of pine and that vast expense of placid, cloud-shredded blue sky?

The peace of the morning put Haggar at rest and infused him with an almost youthful energy. He finished his tea and went back into the cabin to put on his Adidas jogging shoes and brown-and-gold sweat suit. The route he would jog was familiar to him: down the lane, then south on a narrow dirt path that led over a small creek and wound along gentle slopes of dense green woods. It was the sort of route that removed the monotony from his daily jog. At times he hardly noticed how far he'd run or that his breathing was labored. There was only the soft double pat of his feet on the packed earth, and the sun-warmed path before him.

It took Haggar only a few minutes to prepare himself for jogging. But before leaving, he walked into the kitchen and stood in his zippered sweat suit before the open cabinets.

There were only half a dozen cans on the shelves, mostly soups. Some dried fruit, tea, a jar of instant coffee and an unopened tin of imported bacon. On impulse, to put an unpleasant necessary task out of his mind, Haggar found a scrap of paper and quickly made a grocery list of all he would need for the next week. Then he weighted the list with an empty ceramic salt shaker on the counter top and left. He didn't bother locking the door behind him.

He would have done so had he suspected that his decision to seclude himself was made a day late. Haggar already had been targeted as Capp's next victim, and he had been carefully watched by Raul.

Raul had followed Haggar to Lexington and he knew now where the cabin was located. He had talked to Capp on the phone the previous day. His orders were to wait.

Haggar managed two miles but was walking slowly with his hands on his hips when he returned to the cabin. He was careful to jog in moderation. He had a history of heart trouble and his doctor had cautioned him while approving of his jogging. If he didn't overexert himself, the daily jog might be his best medicine.

As he entered the cabin, Haggar wiped the perspiration from his face with his forearm. His damp hair hung in lank, uneven strands on his forehead. Still breathing hard, he walked to one of the chairs by the red conical fireplace and sat down. He was totally relaxed, pleasantly weary, so he tilted back his head, slouched down comfortably in the soft chair and let himself doze.

He awoke near noon to a strange scratching sound.

Haggar sat up straight, blinking, and tried to determine where the sound was coming from. Finally he decided that it came from above and was probably a squirrel on the roof.

As Haggar stood, he realized that he shouldn't have let himself doze. His back was stiff, and one elasticized cuff of his jogging suit had worked up on his wrist to cut off circulation. He shook the numbness from his left hand and knew that if he sat back down he wouldn't want to get up.

After a shower in the cabin's compact bathroom, he felt much better. He put on moccasins, a faded pair of blue jeans and a long-sleeved pullover knit shirt. Then he got his grocery list from the kitchen and added pipe tobacco to it. Folding the list and slipping it into a hip pocket of his jeans, he went outside and got into the Cadillac.

Dust hung in a gritty, lazily settling haze behind the car as Haggar drove along the dirt lane toward the alternate road and the highway that led to Lexington.

He curbed the car finally at a strip shopping center on Margate Avenue in a busy section of town. The centerpiece of the shopping strip was a large colonial-pillared supermarket that would supply everything Haggar needed and perhaps a few of the more exotic foods that he liked.

He got a wire cart just inside the market's pneumatic doors and maneuvered through the crowd near the checkout counters. The cart had a flat spot on one wheel that caused it to clatter as it rolled. Haggar couldn't remember ever choosing a grocery cart without a flat spot on one wheel, and idly he wondered if they were manufactured that way.

As he worked his way through the wide aisles and passed a pyramided canned corn display, Haggar glimpsed a tall Latin-featured man near the baking supplies. The man had hulking shoulders and large brown eyes. He was wearing brown slacks and a tan windbreaker, and he was disturbingly familiar to Haggar.

The man moved on, but Haggar was sure he'd seen him somewhere before. If only he could get another look at him.

But when Haggar detoured around two preoccupied female shoppers and reached the end of the aisle, the man was nowhere in sight. The vague apprehension he thought he'd left behind began to coil into knots in Haggar's stomach.

But it was ridiculous. No one could know he was here—at least no one he had to fear. He'd told Wellman his whereabouts in case an emergency arose, but all even Wellman had was the phone number of a nearby service station. The cabin had no phone.

Haggar moved toward the check-out counters and after a short wait in line paid for his groceries. He carried the two full brown paper bags to the Cadillac and placed them in the trunk. Twice he turned suddenly, hoping to see the man in the tan windbreaker.

Imagination, he assured himself. But he didn't feel like driving directly back to the cabin. Instead he drove downtown.

Haggar parked the car in a lot that charged a dollar for the first hour. Then he began to walk the busy streets. It wasn't yet one o'clock, and employees on their lunch hours still created heavier than normal traffic.

When he stopped to examine the window of a men's clothing store, Haggar moved as if to enter the store, then turned abruptly as if he'd changed his mind. For an instant he saw the man in the tan jacket, just before the man turned his back and disappeared into a doorway or alley.

It had all happened so fast it might have been an illusion.

Raul knew he'd been seen by Haggar, twice if only briefly. And Haggar was spooked; he was no novice and was difficult to follow if on his guard. There was nothing to do but stay with him, give him as long a lead as possible.

Cautiously Raul moved out from the alley he'd ducked into when Haggar looked back. Haggar was farther down the street now, walking at a fast pace toward where he'd left his car.

Raul sidestepped a pair of yammering young girls and quickened his pace to keep up.

Near a bookshop on Nocturn Street, Haggar turned the corner without looking back. When Raul reached the corner Haggar was almost out of sight, walking at a clip just short of a run. Haggar turned right and disappeared. Raul cut down the street nearest him; he would either keep pace with Haggar or intercept him if he turned right again.

But Haggar was nowhere in sight.

Raul knew he must have doubled back. The Cuban wheeled and ran back the way he'd come, barely in time to see Haggar beyond a group of pedestrians a few blocks away. Raul began walking very fast, aware of the increased rasping of his breath. Haggar glanced back and might have seen him.

Veering left, Haggar crossed the street with the light. Raul ran to the corner when Haggar had passed out of sight. When Raul crossed the street, he saw that he'd closed the distance between pursued and pursuer.

Walking swiftly along the sidewalk of a wide busy street, Haggar stayed near the buildings' unbroken brick walls, clinging to their cruel illusion of protection. He was almost a block ahead of Raul. If Haggar knew for sure who Raul was—and Raul had to assume that Haggar did—then Raul had no choice but to act as soon as possible. Capp had approved that alternate course of action.

Tires squealed on cement and a horn blasted in front of Raul. At the corner, Haggar had crossed the busy street against the traffic light, then had broken into a run. Raul could only parallel the move farther down the block. He stepped off the curb, straining to see so he could be sure Haggar was continuing on a straight course. It appeared as if—

The speeding car in the curb lane struck Raul squarely in the backs of his legs, buckling his body and dropping him in the car's path. The woman driving the car had two children with her. Everyone was screaming as Raul's body thudded, buffeted between the pavement and the car's underside. The woman panicked, and it took her almost half the block to stop the car and sit sobbing hysterically over the steering wheel while her blond, pale children stared wide-eyed out the back window.

Haggar stopped running and entered the revolving door of a department store. He tried to force calm on himself. He wasn't actually sure if the man behind him was the same man he'd glimpsed in the supermarket. It could be that the only thing he was running from was imagination.

Pretending to examine a rack of ties, Haggar stood watching the store's entrance.

A steady stream of customers entered and exited, among them a young Catholic priest. Long ago, in his childhood, Haggar had been a devout Catholic, and though he hadn't been inside a church in many years, he felt an almost overwhelming impulse to stop the priest and talk to him. But he stood silently by the tie rack and from the corner of his eye saw the priest disappear into sporting goods.

Five minutes passed, by Haggar's perspiration-loosened wristwatch. And the man in the tan jacket didn't enter the store. Possibly he was waiting outside for Haggar to emerge.

But Haggar knew that wasn't likely. The store surely had another exit, and the man would have no way of knowing which way Haggar would leave. Procedure was to follow the quarry into any large establishment with more than one exit. If the man knew procedure. If there was a man.

Haggar left by a side exit, got his bearings and walked slowly, watchfully, back to where his car was parked.

There was no sign of the man in the tan jacket.

Raul hadn't phoned in.

Capp was eating a carryout hamburger in the motel room when he heard the early news report on the radio:

An unidentified man who appeared to be of Latin descent

was struck and killed by a car this afternoon on Hoover Avenue. The man was stepping off the curb in the middle of the block when he was struck. He died almost instantly and a search of his pockets revealed no identification. Anyone having information concerning the man's identity is asked to notify the police department as soon as possible.

In Egypt—

Capp switched off the radio, realized he was holding his half-eaten hamburger and set it down on the dresser top. The scent of the cooked beef was suddenly nauseating.

Raul was dead . . .

Had Haggar managed it somehow? It wasn't likely; Raul was twice the pro that Haggar had been. And Haggar couldn't have been alerted.

Then a simple auto accident. But surely Haggar was involved. And if he wasn't involved, he might soon see a picture of Raul on television or in a local paper.

Capp sat hunched on the edge of the bed and folded his arms across his stomach. Something with the weight and density of stone seemed to plummet within him. He'd been responsible for men's deaths before, but Raul had been a friend. Capp realized he'd let Raul become too much of a friend.

Raul knew the rules, Capp thought grimly as he stood up and tucked in his shirt. *Raul knew the rules.*

Capp slung his jacket over his shoulder and went outside to where his car was parked. The bile of regret lay bitter at the back of his throat.

☒ 18

STARING FIXEDLY AHEAD at the rushing highway, Haggar drove back toward the turnoff to his cabin. Maybe it was wrong, he was thinking. Maybe what some of the papers said about what they had done was true. Who could recognize evil in the world we lived in today? Berwin, Stauker, Whitencroft, maybe all of them were evil incarnate and didn't know it. Would they know it? Would he know it?

Haggar made himself ease his foot off the accelerator and concentrate on his driving. Steep pine-covered hills flanked the car on either side, and the highway began to wind. The inside of the Cadillac was silent, calming. There was only the occasional soft singing of tires on cement as Haggar took a curve.

His arrival at the cabin, in so simple and beautiful a setting, was like a benediction. Here he was safe.

He parked the car at the side of the porch and sat for a moment absorbing the surrounding tranquillity, the infrequent trill of a bird, the ticking of the cooling engine. Then he got out of the car, removed the groceries from the trunk and carried them inside.

After putting away the groceries, Haggar walked into the cabin's main room, went to the bar and poured himself two fingers of brandy. He sat on the small sofa and sipped his drink, almost convinced now that he'd been fleeing a product of his fears. There had been a man in the supermarket who looked vaguely familiar, and the fact that he might have been Cuban—there had been so many Cuban expatriates involved in Gateway—had inflamed Haggar's imagination. Then, on the street, another man in a tan jacket. That had been all that was needed to panic Haggar. Now, sipping his brandy in the quiet of the cabin, he couldn't help remembering the biblical adage "The wicked flee when no man pursueth." Undeniably, Haggar had fled.

When he'd finished his drink, Haggar found that he was restless. He stood and paced for a few minutes, poured himself another but left it untouched.

Walking into the kitchen, he saw that the early-evening sun had just begun to lengthen the shadows along the lane. He picked up an apple and stood absently munching, staring out the window and down the peaceful rutted lane. A gentle breeze barely stirred the uppermost small branches of the trees, causing a rhythmic faint movement of shadow below. Haggar tossed his apple core into the wastebasket and decided to work off his remaining tension with a short jog before dinner.

After changing into his sweat suit, he laid out the partially defrosted steak he intended to broil later that evening. He would have a simple lettuce-with-dietetic-dressing salad along with the steak, with some of the expensive Burgundy he'd bought.

He left by the rear door, walked for several hundred feet to loosen up, then began an easy, steady jog.

After a mile he was breathing heavily, hypnotized by the rhythmic *p-tup, p-tup, p-tup* of his jogging shoes on the hard earth. He felt the sudden strain on his thighs as he began the long upgrade that rose to the side of the hill behind the cabin. The cabin was a mile and a half away from this point. Haggar carefully adjusted his pace and kept his breathing as smooth as possible. About him lay the deep green quiet of the woods.

Then he was out of the cool woods, and for a long distance ahead the meandering path crossed tilted pasture land that ran to the base of the hills. The gentle breeze stirred indecipherable patterns in the tall grass, and the evening sun was suddenly, surprisingly hot. Perspiration began to sting the corners of Haggar's eyes.

Without breaking stride, he wiped his eyes with a quick motion of his forearm, and as he did so he inadvertently turned his head.

For an instant he glimpsed something moving through the trees behind him.

Haggar glanced back with every other step, the dusty rhythm of his footfalls broken. He was sure he'd seen someone. His breathing became more labored. If anyone was running along the path behind him, pursuing him, they must soon emerge from the trees.

Haggar gasped as a figure did emerge from the cover of the woods, a man in dark slacks and a short-sleeved shirt; a familiar man, running easily at a pace slightly faster than Haggar's own. The man was in top condition, obviously intent on catching up with Haggar. Quickening his pace, Haggar swiveled his head between strides to catch another look at him.

It was Capp! Wilson Capp!

Any doubt as to what really had happened to Drake and Wezenski disappeared from Haggar's mind. Any doubt that he actually had been followed from the supermarket that afternoon was erased by a wash of terror. He strained to run faster, alarmed by the abrupt rasping of his agonized breathing. It was still over a mile to the cabin.

For a long time Haggar didn't look back, holding a steady, fast pace and trying to ignore the dull pain that was shooting up his shins with each step, the increasing ache of his weakening thighs.

When he did look back, he found that Capp had almost halved the distance between them and was still running with a relentless, purposeful ease. There was something smoothly mechanical and terrifying in that stride, something unmistakably predatory.

Haggar opened up his own stride and felt his heart pound vibrantly. He was weakening, occasionally staggering, breathing in broken, shrill gasps that were almost whimpers.

Capp drew nearer.

There was no one, *no one*, in sight who might help. Only high grass and distant wooded hill.

Haggar's heart seemed to explode with each step, and with each explosion pain burned in his chest and radiated in agonizing streaks into his shoulders and down his left arm. He could hear Capp's measured, inexorable footfalls behind him. Or were they echoes of his own faltering steps?

To his right Haggar could now see the cabin's steeply pitched roof. He clenched his teeth and prayed for more strength.

And for an instant the strength was there. Haggar took half a dozen long, determined strides.

Then the pain in his chest spiraled like constricting steel bands about his torso, knifed outward so that his left arm extended stiffly and awkwardly at his side. He could hear and feel the rubber toes of his jogging shoes scraping in the dust as he tried desperately to lift his feet higher but couldn't.

The pain in his chest turned in on itself, gaining strength and substance. A violent series of spasms ran through Haggar's body. Horrified, he realized that he was no longer running. The gritty taste of dust was on his tongue. He was on the ground, paralyzed. The pain disintegrated him, absorbed him, sweeping him through whirling red vortexes that clouded his mind and vision.

Breathing deeply, evenly, Capp stood over the fallen, contorted figure before him on the dusty path. He knew that Haggar was suffering a heart attack.

Haggar's brown sweat shirt had worked its way up to beneath his rigid arms, and one leg was twisted beneath the other. His eyes were open, focused heavily on Capp, and his lips were moving in a writhing pantomime of speech. Capp knelt and placed his ear near Haggar's mouth.

". . . Father," Haggar said distinctly, and his fingertips

brushed the toe of Capp's shoe. ". . . forgive . . ." A momentary dizziness almost prompted Capp to sit down.

He stood up and backed a step.

". . . Lazarus," Haggar murmured.

The biblical figure Christ had raised from the dead. Capp realized that Haggar thought he was a priest.

Haggar attempted to say something more, to beg for absolution, but the writhing dry lips were suddenly stilled, as if they'd become an image on stopped film. The lowering gold sun glinted dully in a lifeless eye.

Capp stood for a moment with his fists on his hips, his chest heaving as his breathing evened out. Around him everything seemed motionless and two-dimensional, seemed somehow to have taken on Haggar's lifelessness.

Capp walked away from Haggar and veered to cut through the woods to where his car was parked.

Haggar would receive no absolution from Capp.

Capp's passage through the woods was easy. There was very little underbrush beneath the dense green trees. When he reached the dirt road, he scrambled up a shallow embankment and crossed to the clearing where the dusty gray compact was barely visible through low, leafy branches.

Seated behind the steering wheel, Capp waited before starting the engine. A throbbing sensation racked his stomach. It was irrational of him to experience even the slightest twinge of pity for Mark Haggar.

Capp knew that he wasn't all that far from Wesville, from where he'd spent the past four years of his life in prison. Where often in his cell he'd thought about Alanna Stauker.

He'd read in the newspaper about Alanna's death, two days after it happened. Her station wagon had run off a desolate Texas highway at high speed and been demolished as it caromed off a utility pole and rolled end over end on hard, rocky ground. Apparently a spark had ignited spilled gasoline, for the wreckage had burned itself out before being discovered.

It had taken a while to identify the charred body as that of Alanna Stauker, wife of one of the Washington kingpins being drawn into the ruinous whirlpool of the Gateway Trust break-in investigation. Another surprise had occurred when almost one hundred thousand dollars was found hidden in the car's spare-tire compartment, where the flames hadn't reached.

Authorities had never determined what caused the accident, nor had the Gateway Senate Investigative Committee ever really proved where the money had come from. But though proof was lacking no one doubted that the money was part of the million and a half dollars unexpectedly found when Capp and his men had broken into Senator Ennis Cordane's Gateway Trust safety-deposit box—bribe money, kickback money, money that would never be fully explained.

As ordered, Capp had turned the contents of the box over to David Wellman, who also was surprised by the illicit windfall.

Subsequent investigation proved that much of the money had been funneled into Berwin's reelection campaign. Shortly before the break-in, Senator Cordane had died of cancer, so the money was thought to be reasonably safe to use. The problem was in where and how to use it. *So much money,* Drake had testified. *We had it, suddenly and unexpectedly. We didn't know what to do with it.*

And as big money is wont to do, this money had left a trail. And the trail had led at least by implication to the White House.

Berwin's resignation had left so many unanswered questions. But Capp was sure that the administration had ordered Alanna's death, possibly even with Dwayne Stauker's approval. She was too expert a driver to be involved in such a convenient accident. What Alanna was doing with the hundred thousand dollars was still unknown. She had always been an opportunist, a survivor; maybe she'd run with some of the money. Maybe she was going to meet Stauker somewhere in South America. Whatever had happened, she was dead.

A small brown rabbit, lean and coiled in the deformity of its hop, bolted across the clearing and disappeared in the rough high brush beyond the hood of the car. The sight of the wary animal suddenly brought home to Capp the fact that his tranquil green surroundings masked the familiar grim struggle of life and death. One survived in any manner or was devoured.

Capp started the engine, backed out onto the rutted dirt road and drove for the highway.

☒ 19

"MARK HAGGAR IS DEAD," Myra said. She was standing in the entry hall with a curious sort of forward balance, as if almost weightless. In her right hand was the evening paper that had been tossed onto the lawn of their home a few minutes before.

Capp looked up in feigned surprise from reading *People and the Penal Code.* He was seated in the living room, wearing tan leather moccasin slippers and nursing the bourbon and water on the table beside him. "Dead how?"

"A heart attack," Myra said, studying the paper. Her relief at finding the cause of death to be natural passed like a reflection over her face as she glanced at Capp. Not that there weren't ways . . .

"Three of us now," Capp said, "and in such a short time." He was sure that the "us" would further allow Myra to assuage her suspicions, as she so desperately wanted to do. Through the years he had learned to play expertly and consciencelessly on her penchant for self-delusion.

Myra walked all the way into the living room, carrying the folded paper at her side, and sat opposite Capp on the sofa. Haggar's death was bold-print front-page news. Capp could make out the words "found dead." He didn't want to ask Myra for the paper too quickly.

She sat reading silently, leafing to the inside page where the account of Haggar's death was continued.

"I'll look at it when you're done," Capp told her. He knew better than to pretend total disinterest. He lowered his gaze again as if reading his book.

Myra had been listening to the radio in the kitchen and had left it playing. Strains of a concert pianist's mad rendition of a Rachmaninoff concerto lent an out-of-sync, frantic accompaniment to the outwardly peaceful scene in the Capp living room.

"He'd had a history of heart trouble," Myra said, adjusting the position of the spread newspaper so the light from the window didn't shine through it.

"Then I suppose what happened shouldn't be surprising. Haggar was in his mid-fifties."

"Fifty-three."

"That's a time of life when you think you're in better condition than you're in," Capp said.

"And the strain of the last several years. He was vacationing at his cabin in Kentucky when he died."

"Alone?"

"Yes, according to what it says here."

"Too bad," Capp replied. "If there'd been somebody else there maybe they could have done something."

"I doubt it. This says it must have been sudden."

"Maybe the heat."

"No, Will, he was inside the cabin."

Capp turned a page of his book. Warning signals honed by years of experience came alive.

As Myra refolded the paper she glanced at her husband. He did seem genuinely concerned. She knew enough to read small signs.

Myra laid the folded newspaper within Capp's reach on the sofa and rose to go back into the kitchen. Capp didn't pick up the paper right away. From the corner of her vision Myra saw him take a slow sip of his drink.

When Capp was alone, he dog-eared a page to mark his place in his book, set the book aside and picked up the newspaper.

Myra had read correctly. Two youthful hikers had knocked on Haggar's cabin door for directions, got no response and peered in through a window before leaving. They had seen Haggar's body on the floor near the center of the main room and left, thinking that he might be asleep or drunk.

But conscience had finally compelled them to contact the sheriff's office, and a sheriff's deputy had investigated and found Haggar dead.

It wasn't a matter of a typographical error or a stray piece of misinformation; it appeared that Haggar definitely had been found inside the cabin.

Capp sat with the paper in his lap, dark eyes intent but unfocused, pondering. For the sake of thoroughness he would double-check the story with other news reports, but he was sure it was accurate, at least on the broad point of where the body was discovered. How could Haggar's body have been returned to the cabin? What did it mean? Capp had seen enough death to know that Haggar was dead on the path. That he might have had some residue of life in him and recovered enough to make his way back to the cabin, then died on the floor, was impossible. Death had set itself about him like a shroud.

The affair raised questions about Raul's death, and would raise more questions when Raul was identified, as he must be soon. Had his death been part of another player's plan? Capp dismissed that idea. He had seen TV news coverage of the mother and her two children who were in the car when it struck Raul. Their grief and shock couldn't have been faked. And Raul had precipitated the accident. Witnesses said that he'd unaccountably stepped hurriedly into the street in the middle of the block, veered as if on impulse to meet a hastily determined fate.

A cool sort of cautiousness took root in Capp's mind, a healthy survivor's wariness that broadened and sharpened his senses. He reached for his drink, but instead of lifting the glass to his lips simply stared into it, absently shifting the ice cubes from side to side with a repetitive clinking sound.

The situation had developed new dangers.

And had taken on a new fascination.

☒ 20

CHERENO HAD SAND in his shoe.

He walked silently beside Berwin along the beach. Berwin was walking on the ocean side and seemed to taunt the surf as his footprints veered in casual variations from a straight course. A distant ship was visible on the horizon against low-lying grayish clouds, and a few gulls wheeled and screamed as if warning of impending rain. At times the spent waves reached to within inches of Berwin's polished black shoes, then drew back. Chereno wished Berwin would get tired and turn back toward the house.

"I can't say that I agree with your actions," Berwin said, thoughtfully but with a distinct trace of disappointment.

"I wouldn't have looked for him at all," Chereno said. "Only when I let myself into the cabin I saw a frozen steak thawing on the sink counter. Haggar's car was parked outside and there were no tracks from another vehicle, so I figured he had to be around."

"And you found him dead on the path."

A stiff wind from the gulf whipped Chereno's unbuttoned sport coat. He found himself parodying Berwin as he jammed his hands into his coat pockets, his shoulders hunched. "I was fairly certain it was a coronary. I know the signs. But there are ways of simulating heart attacks."

Berwin was staring down at the damp, pocked sand. "Were there any footprints near the body?"

"No, but the earth was too hard there to take impressions. I decided to move the body to the cabin. I figured if Haggar was murdered, whoever killed him might assume that he'd somehow recovered from near-death and made his way back there. They had to have been seen by him, so they'd have to attempt to finish the job. Only I'd be waiting in the cabin. It seemed like a possibility I couldn't pass up."

"But now the killer knows he's being pursued by someone other than the law," Berwin pointed out.

"If Haggar was murdered."

"Oh, he was murdered. My instincts tell me that. I've always trusted my instincts."

There were comments Chereno might have made, but he wisely chose not to. "After a few hours those kids came along and banged on the door, peeked in the windows. I had no choice but to leave."

The two men stopped walking as they came to a tall chain link fence topped by angled barbed wire. The fence, set in a low cement wall, crossed the beach and disappeared into the sea, dipping out of sight some hundred yards offshore. A line of gulls sat on the fence top out over the waves, occasionally taking turns flapping off to circle in tight arcs, then rejoining the discordant chorus. A particularly high wave roared along the line of the fence and all the gulls took flight.

Berwin began walking back the way they had come, almost exactly retracing his shallow footsteps. Chereno walked beside him, his straight dark hair now totally disarrayed by the gusting breeze.

"I suppose there's nothing to do but continue as we were," Berwin said. "Report to me at the prescribed times, and I have the various phone numbers where I can contact you if need be."

"Yes, sir. And if I might suggest, it wouldn't be a bad idea for you to tighten security measures here."

"I've already done that to the degree I think necessary."

Chereno had paid particular attention to the security precautions when he'd arrived. They were tight and sophisticated, but a really skilled and experienced pro, such as might be the person he was tracking, could find openings. Again Chereno deemed it unwise to directly contradict Berwin.

"It seems logical that you're the killer's ultimate intended victim," he said, glancing sideways at Berwin as they walked.

"That isn't a new danger to me," Berwin replied.

Chereno knew that to be true, but this was different. This threat was on a calculated, personal level.

"You forget where I've been," Berwin was saying almost petulantly, "where I've sat."

"No, sir, but there's never been a direct physical attempt on your life."

"That's true," Berwin admitted. "They tried to destroy me with words, rumor and innuendo—knives of twisted truth. And they think they've succeeded. Believe me, that kind of attack can be just as real as what we're guarding against here, just as deadly. But if you do your job with the experience I know you possess, any threat can be deterred, crushed before it achieves real potency."

"Yes, sir." The pitch of Berwin's voice had risen. Chereno wished they would reach the house.

Berwin said nothing more. Both men walked silently, the hushed suction of their footsteps in damp sand the only sound in the intervals between rushing waves.

Chereno knew he had little choice but to follow Berwin's orders. During the administration, Stauker, who had then been director of the CIA, had Chereno perform some personal and highly confidential functions for President Berwin. That some of these functions were illegal had at the time seemed irrelevant.

It had begun when Chereno became involved in a project designed to plant in the news media damaging information concerning potentially strong political rivals. As the project expanded, those involved discovered how easy it was to manipulate the media, and ironically it was especially easy if the story to be planted had no basis in fact whatsoever. In those instances, while there was nothing to substantiate, there also were fewer solid leads whereby a story could be fully investigated and disproved. Chereno had been largely responsible for the project's rather surprising degree of success.

Then had come the Kramer affair. Wade Kramer was a western senator who had voiced opposition to many of Berwin's methods and perceptions of the office of president. Kramer had entered the primaries, and while given no chance for the nomination in July, he threatened to raise embarrassing questions and possibly cut substantially into Berwin's popularity.

A young man in Chicago had written several threatening and obviously irrational letters to Kramer, which the senator dutifully had turned over to the FBI along with the regular ration of candidate's hate mail. Theodore Russo had been the disturbed young man's name, and after careful consultation with agency psychiatrists, Stauker had secretly chosen Russo from a long list of possibilities.

Russo's letters were intercepted, and Chereno would answer them by phone. Usually the anonymous phone calls were made late at night, so that it was seldom that Russo obtained a full eight hours' sleep. And while Russo was at work, Chereno had gained access to his small, trash-littered apartment, seen the crude scrawled lettering on the walls and read the agonized notebooks and diary. And Chereno had added to the lettering, altered the notebooks and diary, left "signs" in the apartment that were later referred to in the late-night phone calls. Not once had Russo inquired about Chereno's identity; within a few calls he had come to accept Chereno's softly modulated voice as an extension of his own.

The purpose of it all was to get Russo actually to carry out his threat to assassinate Kramer when the senator's itinerary brought him to Chicago.

Russo had responded, and afterward he'd told about the voices and the signs. The public was used to that kind of talk; it was the ranting of an obviously schizophrenic and dangerous individual.

One bullet had missed, the other had smashed into Kramer's spine when he'd spun to avoid it. Kramer wasn't killed, but he was permanently crippled and rendered an ineffective campaigner. Another Chereno success.

Chereno's next major assignment had been Alanna Stauker. It had been easy to force her station wagon off the desolate road, to walk back and ignite the wreckage. But not thinking to look in the spare-tire compartment for the money was inexcusable. Chereno had borne the brunt of the consequences of that oversight. He had been placed on the shelf and left there until Berwin's recent invitation to Lost Palms.

Chereno had kept his mouth shut about the Alanna Stauker affair, not attempting to defend himself. And that had been wise. It had been Stauker himself who had ordered her death, when after a violent argument she'd run with money and potent information. But Berwin knew about it. Berwin knew about everything that went on during those years.

As they climbed the rough wooden steps that led up from the beach, Berwin said, "I'm sure you realize that if everything goes well you'll be justly rewarded."

"I appreciate that, sir."

Chereno knew that Berwin would stand by his words. Reward and punishment were an important ingredient of the Berwin political philosophy.

When they reached the house, Berwin did not invite Chereno inside.

The two men shook hands, and Chereno walked to where his five-year-old blue Dodge sedan was parked. There was a large dent in the car's left front fender that he'd never bothered to have repaired. As Chereno shut the car's door, he glanced over to see that Berwin was standing watching him.

Berwin's angular, graceless figure appeared for an instant in the rearview mirror as Chereno started the car and turned sharply onto the blacktop drive.

Chereno drove the short distance to the gate, stopped and waited while the shirt-sleeved guard worked the controls that swung the large section of the fence well to the side to clear the road. Then Chereno drove to the check-out point by the main gate, which was open. He slowed and waved to a similarly dressed guard. Without smiling, the guard nodded and waved him through. Chereno accelerated along the smooth, straight road that led to the highway.

A circling gull had left an astoundingly large and viscous mess on the car's windshield.

That seemed a bad omen.

☒ 21

RAUL ESTEBEN'S BODY had been identified through his fingerprints. The proximity of his death to Haggar's death had been remarked on during the TV network news. No one, including Raul's widow in Philadelphia, seemed to know what he was doing in Lexington, Kentucky.

But Capp knew Marie Esteben, knew that she suspected more than she was saying. She was the sort of woman who would be as loyal to her husband now as when he was alive. At least as long as she could be sure of what he would have wanted.

Capp would have to talk to her. He needed her silence.

Early the next afternoon, Capp was in Philadelphia. He crossed Vector Street, entered the old four-story brick apartment building and climbed three flights of narrow, linoleumed stairs to Marie Esteben's door. The pungent, mingled cooking smells common to apartment buildings wafted in the air. In one of the apartments below Capp, a man and woman were arguing vehemently. The walls needed painting so badly they seemed resigned to drabness, and some of the graffiti scrawled on them was in Spanish.

Capp reached the top of the stairs, walked along the uneven floor of the hall to the Esteben apartment's door. He knocked and stood looking around him at more peeling paint, a cracked hall window and a bare ceiling bulb. Raul had been ill treated by the world since prison.

Marie was wearing a plain black dress and low-heeled

black shoes when she answered the door. Her dark hair was parted in the middle and pulled back away from her face. Capp had phoned and she was expecting him. She looked at him with neither friendliness nor hostility and invited him inside.

The interior of the apartment was what Capp expected to see in such a building, but here and there existed pathetically determined efforts to add cheer. But there was no real cheer. The colorful touches had taken on the aura of a clown's sad, brightly painted face.

Marie motioned for Capp to sit on the worn sofa and sat down herself in a facing chair. She primly crossed her legs and rested pale, very still hands in her lap. In a gaunt, noble sort of way she was quite beautiful, possessing what a casting director would consider good facial bones.

"I suppose you're here to offer condolences," she said.

Capp nodded. "Will you accept them, Marie?"

A smile that excluded him. "At this point it makes little difference."

"There's something else," Capp said.

"I was sure there would be."

"Raul was working for me when he was killed."

"It had to be."

"But I'm sure his death was unconnected with what he was doing for me. It was a simple accident."

Marie shook her head. "It wasn't a simple accident, it was because he was a fool. As you are."

"There's a great deal you don't know, that I can't tell you."

"And I don't want to know. Because I don't care. Because it's unimportant." She was leaning forward now and her dark eyes were large and painted with light. Then she sat back. "I loved Raul," she said softly, as if there'd been some doubt. For another woman the scene might have been a prelude to tears, but Marie wasn't about to cry.

"Why is what Raul was doing unimportant, Marie?" Capp asked.

"Because it's meaningless. In the long run, it changes nothing."

"You're wrong, Marie. It matters."

"Only to people like you and Raul."

Capp squirmed slightly on the sofa, vaguely unsettled. "Meaningless in the long run, you say, but what do you propose for the short run?"

"A concern with more personal happiness."

Capp walked to the open window and looked down at the squalor of the street three stories below. "A pleasant but naïve dream, Marie. They won't let you concentrate on matters closest to your personal well-being."

"You are 'they.'"

Capp turned to face her, haloed by the light at his back. "You seem to have given it all a lot of thought."

"I had to. I knew my husband was a fool living in a fool's world. It's a world that feeds on itself, and soon things within it take on an urgency that doesn't exist outside that world. But the fools within need desperately for it to be that way."

Capp returned to the sofa and sat down. He was tired of listening to Marie. He could imagine her and Raul sitting up into the dawn hours over wine and crackers, talking college bull session philosophy. And now she was drawing Capp into her world of doubt and cynicism.

"I know why you came," she said.

"Do you?"

But Capp knew that she did. It bothered him that she was so perceptive and held the views she had just expressed.

"You need my silence. To protect yourself."

"Exactly," Capp said. Marie possessed the sort of astuteness that made almost anyone dealing with her choose candor as the wisest course. "Do I have your silence?"

"You do."

Capp looked at her, into the quiet, knowing depths of her dark eyes. She was one of those women whose beauty seems to increase with each glance. "Why?" he asked. "If it's all meaningless?"

"Because Raul would have wanted it that way, and I honor his memory. And because I know you're not to blame for his death so much as he is." Her pale hands, curiously aged, began an unconscious weaving motion in her lap. "I actually know very little, only that you and he were involved in something. The rest would be conjecture on my part."

"What I don't want is for anyone to learn that I've contacted Raul since prison," Capp said.

"They won't. Not from me."

He believed her. There was about Marie a sad and simple honesty that assured Capp he could take her at her word.

Capp stood up but Marie remained seated.

"I want you to believe that I'm sorry, Marie," he said, looking down into her steady, resigned gaze. For the first time he noticed the pink-tinted signs of crying about her eyes.

"I believe you, Wilson. I was about to eat lunch, some sandwiches. Do you care to have lunch with me?"

"No, it would be better if I left."

She nodded solemnly, as if she knew the meaning of his words better than he did.

Capp went to the door. "Raul was lucky to have you," he said. "You both were lucky."

"Everyone is lucky and a fool."

"You make it sound like dime-store philosophy, but maybe it's true."

She said nothing more to him so he went out.

Capp walked down the hall and descended the narrow, dim stairs. A door slammed on the floor beneath him and a baby began to cry. The man and woman who had been arguing when Capp entered were still arguing but in more subdued tones. ". . . Forever!" Capp heard the woman say with quiet fierceness as he reached the landing and continued down. He was glad when he reached the street.

Yet, standing in the sunlight, for a few seconds Capp felt a powerful compulsion to go back upstairs and see Marie Esteben again. Her presence, her simple convictions and insights, had been oddly reassuring to him. Almost like a mother's presence.

Capp crossed the street and walked toward Enrico's at Twelfth and Gratton, where he and Raul had met after Capp's release from prison.

When Capp reached Enrico's, he stood for a moment in the paneled foyer, then decided that he wasn't hungry and would have a few drinks rather than lunch. He walked across soft carpet into the dimly lighted lounge crowded with people who were on their lunch hour and awaiting tables.

All the booths and tables were occupied, but Capp found space at the long bar. A well-dressed man next to him was talking loudly about the life-and-death importance of an advertising contract being renewed. A small diamond ring on the man's little finger glittered brightly as he gestured for emphasis. Capp squeezed sideways past the man, sat on a bar stool and ordered a draft beer.

While he waited for his drink he sat thinking about his conversation with Marie Esteben. It was difficult for Capp not to feel compassion for Marie. Yet she seemed to feel an equal compassion for *him.*

The beer arrived in a frosted stein and Capp lifted it in a silent toast to Raul.

As Capp drank, a news brief interrupted the soap opera on the color TV. A neatly coiffed blond female newscaster Capp had never seen before announced that Senator Adam Haller had been declared the winner of the California primary by 1,325,420 to 1,152,311 votes.

Someone whooped loudly and there were a few hand claps.

The adman next to Capp slammed his open palm on the bar. "Shit!" he exclaimed in violent disappointment.

It occurred to Capp that 1,325,420 voters would disagree, and that was a lot of disagreement.

☒ 22

WHILE CAPP DRANK in Enrico's, a short, balding man wearing a neat gray suit knocked on Marie Esteben's door. He had a bulbous forehead accentuated by his baldness, and he thrust out a jutting chin as dauntless as his hooded, mild blue eyes. Though Clyde Hawker was in his late forties and carried a substantial middle-age paunch, his face was comparatively unlined, younger than his eyes. His hands were disproportionately large, with tobacco-yellowed splayed fingers, and looked as if they were very strong. He knocked again, louder.

When Marie opened the door he rocked back on his heels and smiled at her. "Marie Esteben?"

She nodded.

"Name's Clyde Hawker. I'm with the FBI." He flashed identification at her. "I'm sorry about your husband."

"Did you know Raul?"

"No. May I come in?"

"Of course." She stepped back politely but with a certain apprehension.

Clyde Hawker entered and glanced around, his almost femininely beautiful smile lingering incongruously on his face. Marie invited him to sit down but he declined.

"Have I interrupted your lunch?" he asked.

"I was finished," she lied. She walked behind a high-backed chair and stood leaning against it, bracing herself with her arms, as if the floor might tilt.

"I'd like to talk to you about your husband," Hawker said.

"Why?"

"We need to know what he was doing in Lexington, Kentucky, the day he was run down."

"For what reason?"

Hawker laughed with genuine amusement and shook his head to indicate that Marie was quite a character. "Seems you'd rather ask than answer. Most people would."

"I don't have the answers, Mr. Hawker."

"Now, Mrs. Esteben, do you mean your husband ran off to Lexington without telling you where he was going or why?"

Marie nodded. She had no reason to lie to Hawker. Raul had always made sure she knew nothing that might endanger either of them. It was only Wilson Capp she had to consider.

"What sort of work did your husband do after his release from prison?" Hawker asked.

"He taught Spanish at two schools. Night classes."

"But he quit those jobs a month ago. Had he been looking for work?"

"I wasn't aware that he'd quit. Raul handled the money."

"I see. Had he been away from home for extended periods before disappearing to Lexington for a week?"

"He would disappear at times. It was his way. And he wasn't gone for a week before he was killed in Lexington."

"Ah, yes, that's true. More like a few days."

"More like that."

"How many days?"

"Three."

"Yes . . . and he took a plane to Lexington."

"Did he?"

"You don't know?"

Marie shook her head. "I woke up, Raul was gone. He'd left a note."

"The note said?"

"That he loved me and would return as soon as possible."

"Your husband was a secretive man, Mrs. Esteben."

"Can you blame him? He remembered being hounded by the press, betrayed and imprisoned."

Hawker reached into his shirt pocket and withdrew a pack of king-sized Kools. "Betrayed?"

"That's how he felt."

"Do you mind if I smoke?"

"Yes."

Hawker continued to hold the Kools but didn't withdraw a cigarette. It was possible that Marie Esteben actually did know very little or nothing. She seemed remotely amused.

"Just how bitter was your husband?" Hawker asked.

"Bitter?" Marie caressed her chin with the backs of her knuckles. "I don't think Raul was bitter. He had a philosophical way of looking at things."

"Ah, that can be a valuable asset in a man."

"Or a fatal flaw."

"Yes, depending on the man." Hawker put the cigarettes back in his pocket, then he stood politely with his hands clasped behind him and his weight evenly distributed on planted feet, a strangely graceful, casual parade rest. "You must understand why I'm asking these questions," he said. "There have been a series of deaths involving former government officials, some of them under federal indictment. And your husband had dealings with these men."

"Years ago, yes."

"You know of whom I'm speaking?"

"Of course. Those involved in Gateway."

"Including your husband, four men who were implicated in Gateway have recently died."

"You think it's not coincidental?"

"Frankly, I don't know. I was hoping you might tell me something that would shed light."

"I'm sorry if I leave you in darkness."

"Light will come, Mrs. Esteben."

"That's an optimistic outlook."

"If you do think of anything that might be of help, I'd appreciate you phoning me at this number." Hawker handed her a white business card. "Then my optimism will be justified."

Marie looked at the card, then laid it on a table near the chipped ceramic base of a lamp. She went with Hawker to the door, noticing as she walked behind him a faint lemon scent that must have come from a cosmetic he was wearing.

"Much thanks for your cooperation," he said, stepping into the hall. He gave her his unexpectedly beautiful smile and was gone, his footsteps clattering down the stairs.

Marie went to the window and waited until Hawker emerged from the building. She watched him cross the street to a small green car, get in, sit for a moment reading something, then drive away. Though he'd never looked up at her, she had the sensation that he knew she was at the window.

Staring down into the empty street, Marie wondered if she should tell Capp about Hawker's visit. She decided there was no reason. Raul was dead. For him, for her, the game was ended.

Marie left the window, crossed the room and absently turned on the portable TV set. She found that on each channel was a report on the California primary results.

She turned off the TV and stood watching the picture shrink to a pinpoint, then disappear as if whirled off into infinity. With her arms crossed tightly so that she was gripping her elbows, she stood by the window. Politics did not interest Marie.

⊠ 23

HE HAD WON.

California was his; the nomination was almost assured.

Senator Adam Haller sat in his cool, plush suite on the twelfth floor of San Francisco's Hyatt Regency Hotel and grinned for the half dozen network newsmen who'd been allowed to enter. His wife Judith sat next to him on the sofa, before the large RCA color TV on which they'd watched the returns. Daughter Emma and teen-age son Graham reclined in nearby chairs, obviously pleased by their father's success and admirably restrained in their expressions of exuberance. Haller hoped that neither of them would suddenly stand and give a victory shout, as Graham had done in Maryland.

Judith was being the candidate's ideal wife, poised, glowing, gracious and with an unmistakable glitter of intelligence. She'd had plenty of practice and had perfected her art of appearing as the public expected. The irony of it was that she actually was the way she tried so hard to appear. The news media had long since sensed that and was firmly on her side.

"On to New York now, Senator?" Ewing of CBS asked from across the room.

Haller allowed his grin to widen. "On to New York." He knew, as they all did, that it was possible for him to lock up the nomination there.

Adam Haller had served sixteen good years in the United States Senate. During that time his boyish features had taken on a handsomely lined look of mature wisdom. The tanned flesh about his gray eyes was crinkled with crow's feet, and wide creases ran from either side of his hawkish nose to the corners of his wide, firm lips. His hairline had receded and his sideburns were shot with gray. Yet he retained a trace of the boyish enthusiasm that had first endeared him to voters.

Unlike that of his wife, Senator Adam Haller's public image didn't quite mesh with his true personality. He was no longer boyish and enthusiastic; he was coldly pragmatic and calculating. He'd found it the only way to survive in politics.

Haller's Senate record was impressive. As a young senator he had introduced practical and at the time controversial civil rights legislation. With seniority he had taken his place on various influential committees, and had always performed with judgment and decorum. In the mid-seventies he had chaired the NACO Energy Committee and had been instrumental in negotiating several strong bills through both houses. And Haller had reluctantly recommended impeachment proceedings against Andrew Berwin when to do so had meant sticking one's political neck out directly over the chopping block. But that particular ax, poised above so many of the worthy, had never fallen.

The phone in Haller's suite was ringing almost continually. Jeremy Page, Haller's campaign manager, was taking most of the congratulatory calls, smiling behind his reddish full beard as he accepted his due for his role in the recent triumph. He put down the receiver and looked over at Haller with a happy, mock-exhausted expression.

"Want to handle the phone for a while, Senator?" he asked.

Haller knew that Jeremy had the personal touch in mind for the benefit of the press. It would make for good TV and newspaper coverage.

"If you're wearing out," Haller said, smiling and pushing his lanky frame out of the soft sofa. He sat by the phone, in the fringed armchair that Jeremy had vacated for him.

The phone rang immediately and Haller lifted the receiver.

"Adam Haller here . . ."

He fielded the calls with aplomb and with benevolence to the vanquished. A gracious winner all the way, who would doubtless be gracious sitting in victory in the White House.

In his suite in the Royalton West, within easy walking distance of Senator Haller's hotel, Senator Walter Temple, runner-up to Haller in the California presidential primary, sat like a pensive monarch among subdued subjects. His entourage was despondent, still adjusting to the reality of defeat.

Temple seemed the least disturbed of anyone in the room. He was a tall, slender man who personified the word *dignified.* His elegant, loquacious exterior concealed the ambition that had driven him for the past twenty years toward the goal he seemingly had lost. For Adam Haller was now undeniably the favorite.

While the large suite was crowded with distraught men and women, most of them holding drinks as they talked in quiet clusters, Temple sat in a chair near a window, sending a ball-point pen gliding over a pad of paper resting on his knee. He tore the top sheet of paper from the pad, clipped the pen in his shirt pocket and waved Willy Shawn, one of his aides, over to where he sat.

"I'd like you to have this sent as a telegram to Senator Haller," he said.

Shawn, a shambling, unkempt man of ruddy complexion and formidable size, accepted the sheet of paper and read:

> Senator Haller:
>
> Sincere congratulations on attaining the plateau we both coveted. However, the peak is not yet reached.
>
> Senator Walter Temple

"There's no need to be upset, Willy," Temple whispered to Shawn. "I have good reason to remain confident."

Millie Germayne, of the *Examiner,* was nearby and couldn't help but overhear.

Shawn nodded. His loosely knotted tie was red and made

his broad face seem especially florid. "It's just that we came so close, Senator. Closer than any of us imagined. It's too bad there wasn't more time for the balance to shift completely." He angled his body sideways and made his way toward a phone to call in the congratulatory telegram.

Lariman of NBC watched as Shawn wove his way toward the phone with the message clutched in his beefy hand. Several other media people had spotted Shawn and were making their way toward the telephone. Lariman nodded to his cameraman and moved toward Temple. He tapped Temple lightly on the shoulder.

"Senator Temple, have you contacted Senator Haller yet?"

"One of my aides is phoning in my congratulatory telegram at this moment," Temple said. He seemed completely at ease and unaffected by his loss.

"How do you see the situation now, Senator?" Lariman asked.

"What situation?" Temple asked with a wink, and there was laughter.

Several other TV people had gathered around Temple's chair. A few of them were jostled from behind and a piece of equipment dropped with a sickening crunch of compacting metal.

"Why don't we go into the other room," Temple invited. "It's quieter and less crowded in there, and I'll be glad to answer your questions." He stood up and the way was parted for him.

In the quiet of the suite's large master bedroom, Temple stood against a background of pleated blue velvet drapes and faced the lights and questions. The newsmen, as befitted their position in their field, were smooth and diplomatic as they probed.

"Do you feel now that your cause is lost, Senator?"

"Oh, not at all, Tom," Temple directly addressed the well-known newsman. "Actually the results of this primary are closer than we'd privately predicted some weeks ago. The gap was closing fast, and given another week or two I'm confident I'd have won here."

"How do you see your chances in New York?"

A knowledgeable, confident smile. "Excellent."

"Will you lend your support to Senator Haller if he becomes the nominee, sir?"

"I don't foresee that eventuality."

"When you take your campaign to New York, Senator, do you plan any changes in your position or in your approach to the voters?"

"I don't believe that's necessary. Given the unexpected closeness of the vote here in California, I think it's obvious that the voters are becoming familiar with the men and issues and the swing to my candidacy is well under way. The outcome here illustrates a momentum that will surely carry me to the nomination and presidency. I don't pretend I wouldn't rather have received the majority vote here, but I mean it when I say that in a sense the outcome can be construed as a victory. It substantiates our belief in a national groundswell of support."

The questions continued for another ten minutes, and Temple continued to answer them with the eloquence, openness and good humor that had characterized his campaign from the first narrow victory in New Hampshire.

When the impromptu press conference was ended, Temple went back into the main room and mingled with his disappointed supporters and campaign workers, reassuring them. He seemed to enjoy talking with them. Eventually the tempo of the conversation quickened, and now and then laughter could be heard. Many of the TV people had left, and Millie Germayne sat next to Senator Temple on the sofa for an exclusive if often interrupted interview.

In their televised analysis of the California campaign, newsmen on all three networks agreed that Senator Temple had suffered a costly but not devastating defeat. They all concluded that the only two candidates of consequence left in the race for the nomination were Walter Temple and Adam Haller. Haller's statement on the aged might yet hurt him in the East and South, and there hadn't yet been time to gauge the reaction to Temple's recently stated position on Canada or to the South African faux pas. On most of the major issues both men's positions were essentially the same. Though there was argument about respective qualifications, the newsmen agreed that the campaign had now come down to a matter of personalities. And it was quite possible that Temple's belief in a narrowing gap in voter sentiment was well founded.

Most of the newsmen taking part in the analysis were impressed by Temple's amazing composure and continued confidence.

☒ 24

Julian Zayas was his usual confident, smiling self when he met Capp by the playground in the park near Capp's home. There were several children playing beneath the tall elms, climbing the iron maze of the jungle gym, hurling themselves down the long curving metal slide, playing a variety of dodge ball with an old lifeless tennis ball against a low brick wall. A skinny boy about twelve, wearing a red sleeveless T-shirt, somehow managed acrobatically to avoid the thrown ball with easy regularity, letting it whack against the bricks and bounce back to the boy who'd thrown it.

Julian was wearing dark slacks and a thigh-length tan jacket with epaulets. He had on yellow-tinted sunglasses of the type that change shades with variances of light. He had phoned earlier and asked to see Capp, leaving a code name with which they were both familiar. Julian had an almost pathological distrust of phones.

He looked about as if pleased by the green grass and towering trees, then said, "In Cincinnati, Wilson, a man has been inquiring about me."

Whack! The tennis ball flattened itself against the unyielding bricks. The boy who had dodged it laughed musically.

"Inquiring where? In what way?" Capp asked.

"Talking to friends, acquaintances, to my brother-in-law Peterson."

"Who does he claim to be with?"

"That's the thing," Julian replied. "He shows no identification, only money."

Whack! More laughter.

"Has he learned anything?"

Julian slowly peeled off the yellow-lensed glasses, like a blind man testing for sight, and shook his head, smiling. "Of course not. No one knows anything to tell him."

A breeze played over the small, flat park, causing the leaves to rustle overhead like the beat of soft wings. Capp walked with Julian to a nearby wood bench. The bench had no back, and both men sat hunched slightly forward.

"Did you get the man's description?" Capp asked.

"No reliable description. Stocky build, wore a hat, no accent." Julian grinned as if at some arcane joke. "You know about the accuracy of descriptions, Wilson."

Capp knew. In the past he had used the knowledge that two witnesses seldom gave the same description. Yet even a vague description eliminated certain pronounced physical characteristics. The man might be any weight from slender to husky, but he wasn't likely to be emaciated or obese. And he had no distinctive visible physical markings such as tattoos or scars that would stick in the mind. The man could be almost anyone, but there were a few people he could not be.

The tennis ball struck the brick wall with a sound like a gunshot. This time the just-missed boy didn't laugh, possibly a bit awed by the surprising force of the impact. He moved up onto the balls of his feet as his opponent's arm drew back for another throw.

"Should we postpone the next one, Wilson?"

Capp stared at the ground and shook his head. "We've covered ourselves carefully. There can be no proof."

"Maybe this man doesn't seek proof."

"Whoever he is, or represents, he'll have to make sure," Capp said. "That will take time. We're going to move ahead."

Julian nodded and rose from the bench, smoothed his pants legs and replaced his sunglasses. "Then we'll meet as planned?"

"Yes," Capp said, also rising. "Let me know, though, if anything else develops. We'll need to start watching our asses with extra care."

"This man has been with us awhile."

"I know," Capp said. "It explains the changed location of Haggar's body. No one knows for sure whether Haggar's coronary was brought about or accidental. It seems our friend might have used the body for bait."

Julian cursed through a humorless grin. "Do you think he killed Raul?"

"No, I think Raul got careless in heavy traffic, possibly while he was trailing Haggar. Maybe Haggar spotted him and tried to shake loose."

Julian frowned but nodded as if in agreement. A girl of about six ran jerkily by, shrieking happily, trailing a brown sweater clutched by one sleeve.

"At any time, Julian, you can back out of this with no strings attached. I've never led you to believe otherwise."

"The last thing I want is to desert you, Wilson. If you hadn't undertaken this, I would have alone, or with Raul. I was waiting for you."

Capp nodded and smiled. He and Julian shook hands.

"Be careful," Capp said.

"And you."

Capp watched Julian's lithe figure cross the grass and turn toward the street. He was often reminded of a prowling feral cat when he watched Julian. There was about the dapper agent that combination of strength and grace that was peculiarly feline.

Capp sat back down on the bench and considered what Julian had told him. Capp could be sure now that someone was attempting to track him down not only to stop his systematic revenge, but to identify and locate him before the law did with the resultant risk that he might tell what he knew to lighten the burden of a murder charge. The other Gateway participants could be reasonably sure that Capp would remain silent as long as he himself had much to lose by talking. The same could be said of several other potential assassins who carried damning information.

If the man in Cincinnati knew what he was doing, eventually the field would narrow to Capp. But that didn't necessarily mean anything could be proven.

Capp heard a popping sound, then a sharp yelp of pain, and looked over to see the boy in the sleeveless T-shirt doubled over and clutching his right side. The tennis ball had struck him audibly in the ribs. Now the boy who'd thrown the ball was laughing with melodious glee as he jogged off to recover it.

As Capp stood and walked from the park, the laughing youth was taking a turn before the wall.

☒ 25

On the same day that Capp and Julian had their conversation in the park, Walter Chereno maneuvered his battered Dodge along a curving, rutted dirt road south of Shreveport, Louisiana. He cursed as the car bottomed when the road dipped suddenly, then he peered ahead through the cyprus trees to see a surprising number of cars parked on a shallow grassy slope. Beyond the cars was a large unpainted barn with a corrugated tin roof. There were a few people standing among the parked cars, but most of the crowd was gathered in and around the looming barn set amid sun-washed green woods. Chereno could see a large exhaust fan revolving up near the roof of the barn. The fan had been crudely mounted in the wood front of the barn and was braced with two angled two-by-four pieces of lumber.

Chereno parked at the end of the farthest row of cars and walked toward the barn. The wide doors stood rolled open on their overhead steel tracks, but the inside of the barn was too dim for anything to be visible except vague outlines of moving figures. A brown-and-white dog in a portable steel mesh cage eyed Chereno with disinterest from the back of a parked station wagon.

By the time Chereno entered the barn, the preliminaries were over and the main attraction was about to begin. Over a hundred people milled about inside the vast barn. Most of the men wore casual clothing, though there were a few with suits and ties. The women were dressed in jeans or slacks, with blouses or pullover shirts, with the exception of three or four who wore obviously expensive pants suits and glittering jewelry. There was a great deal of talk, punctuated by good-natured arguing and the abrupt yet sweetly rhythmic accents of Louisiana Cajuns. The barn did not smell exactly like a barn: the pungent, musty animal odor was altered by the presence of so many perspiring humans and by the sharp scent of tobacco smoke. The big exhaust fan made a repetitious protest between a growl and a squeak as it struggled vainly to draw the thick grayish haze up and out. Some large, ancient electric fans on pedestals were set about the perimeter of the barn near the plank walls, but Chereno could feel no effect of their presence. Beneath the haze of tobacco smoke was warm, motionless air instilled with an unmistakable expectancy.

The focal point of everyone's interest was a square area in the center of the barn, created by ten-by-one boards so that it resembled a child's sandbox. The barn's earthen floor inside the boundary of the boards was covered with a dark-stained, wrinkled sheet of canvas. The square area was about the size of a small boxing ring and was referred to as the pit.

Everyone was inside the barn now, but there was less loud talk, less movement. Chereno heard hushed voices discussing wagers, and money was placed in the hands of bet holders in that unnoticeable manner one sees among people used to handling cash.

At opposite corners of the pit crouched the two handlers and their dogs. The dogs were Staffordshire terriers, or "pit bulls," medium-sized, short-haired dogs with lean rear bodies, massive chests and powerful jaws. They were bred to fight.

The dog nearest Chereno was Tuffy, a bulky brindle whose ears had long since been chewed completely off. He was owned, trained and handled by Al of St. Louis, a wiry, bearded man with compassionate brown eyes and calm, controlled hands. Al quickly wiped his free hand on a leg of his bib overalls as he held the straining Tuffy by the nape of the neck.

Tuffy's opponent was a black-and-white pit bull named Zeb, known as a "brisket biter" for his proclivity to attack that portion of the opposing dog. Zeb's owner and handler was a muscular, shirtless Cajun named DeMet.

Both dogs were finely trained and had never lost a fight. Both trainer-handlers were among the best in the country. Reputations were at stake, and thousands of dollars had been bet on the long-awaited fight. The odds were even.

A charged silence settled over the crowd as the fight was about to begin. Chereno looked around for Jan Perralt. He saw only unfamiliar pale, tense faces, some calculating, some exhilarated, some worried, some impatient—none of them bored. A well-dressed woman near the front of the crowd bent forward as if under the weight of her glittering jeweled necklace, managed to bite her lower lip and smile at the same time. Perralt was nowhere in sight. Aficionado that he was, if he'd been within a hundred miles—five hundred—of where Chereno stood, he would have attended this fight.

The rules of the pit are similar to the antiquated rules of bare-knuckle boxing. When the dogs are locked inactive or one turns away, the handlers take them back to their corners, the referee signals and they "scratch," which means they come out into the pit to fight some more. When a dog fails to scratch, or is mutilated to the point where it dies or its handler concedes, the match is over. It's a noisy affair, with the crowd shouting and gesticulating and the handlers talking to the dogs and to each other.

At a signal from the referee, the dogs were released by their handlers and came together in almost the exact center of the pit. They didn't bark, circle or snap like ordinary dogs; they weren't ordinary dogs at all. Tuffy and Zeb met at full speed with a solid thud that was almost drowned out by the swell of noise from the crowd. The two dogs struggled frantically but warily, seeking firm toothholds in furred flesh.

A roar shook the barn as Tuffy got a firm grip on the loose flesh at the side of Zeb's thick neck and flipped the black-and-white dog onto its back. The two muscular dogs grappled almost like human wrestlers and Zeb regained his footing and bit ineffectually into Tuffy's back. As they strained and circled on the bloody canvas, the dogs emitted low, rolling growls. Their stubbed tails never stopped wagging.

Tuffy gave Zeb's neck a vicious shake and droplets of blood flew out against the boards and into the crowd. Then the powerful jaws lost their hold and Zeb was on top of Tuffy, gnawing into the area between the front legs known as the brisket.

"Hey, gotchoo now, gotchoo now!" DeMet yelled at Al, who was circling behind the struggling dogs. "You bring a shovel to bury that dog?"

"No shovel," Al said simply, looking concerned. "You bring a spatula?"

Tuffy let out a whimper of pain and skittered away, a long gash in his chest. The handlers took the dogs back to their corners.

Al chanted a whispered litany to Tuffy, bending low and gently rocking the dog in time with his words. Both handlers held their dogs two-handed, keeping the front paws off the ground so the powerful animals couldn't get traction on the canvas.

The referee signaled scratch.

The dogs were released and they slammed together again in the center of the pit. Not an ounce of fight had left either of them. A man behind Chereno was yelling hoarsely and unintelligibly. The woman with the jeweled necklace was slowly running her tongue back and forth over her upper lip. Chereno wished the fight would end. He was the only one not completely caught up in it. But then he didn't have a bet down.

This time Tuffy was getting the better of it, dancing nimbly, jaws clamped about the top of Zeb's head while the black-and-white dog writhed to gain the upper position. In lapses of noise from the crowd, the sound of teeth grinding on bone was steady and relentless.

Half an hour passed, and the dogs scratched five more times. The canvas was slippery with blood now, and Tuffy, who had lost the use of his left forepaw in the clasp of Zeb's brutal jaws, was having increasing difficulty maintaining firm footing.

Within another ten minutes, both of Tuffy's front legs were useless and one eye had been gouged. Zeb had the exhausted dog on its back and was gnawing with weary but enthusiastic persistence on Tuffy's bloody underside. At a nod from the referee, the handlers separated the dogs, DeMet using a wooden hammer handle as a lever to pry open Zeb's powerful jaws. Back to respective bloodstained corners.

The referee gave a hand signal. "Scratch!"

Tuffy tried desperately to leave his corner, chest dragging, forepaws limp and useless, rear legs churning with fierce instinct to propel him to battle. The gaping chest wound and torn underside smeared a reddish, snail-like trail of blood on the canvas. His handler stopped the fight.

The sudden silence around the pit was broken by a few curses, then chatter and the sound of shifting feet, relaxing bodies.

Chereno had been impressed. He could understand how some people became fascinated by these dogs. It was obvious that to the combatants fighting on was more important than life itself; for an instant, for those watching the fight, death had been negated.

Later, during a fight between two smaller bitches, Chereno walked outside and saw Tuffy's handler near a blue station wagon. The maimed dog was on a blanket, lying docilely while Al ministered to it.

"Will he make it?" Chereno asked.

"I don't think so." The handler didn't look up.

"A shame."

"I let him fight too long."

"You had to."

"I shouldn't have."

Chereno knelt, plucked a thick strand of grass and began idly chewing on it. "Do you know Jan Perralt?"

The handler was sprinkling something on the dog's open chest wound. "Sure. Most everyone who breeds pit bulls does."

"He isn't here."

"He's in Canada."

"I'm sorry I missed him. We're old gambling buddies. Was he at the last convention in Colorado?"

"He was. And he lost a lot of money betting on a dog that couldn't fight in that rarefied mountain air."

Chereno knelt silently for a long time, watching the handler tend the dog's wounds. He'd learned what he had come to find out.

Jan Perralt had been in charge of one of the White House carpenter units, so named because they were used to shore up the constantly weakening structure of the administration's labyrinth of covert activities. But finally the carpenters had reached the limit of what shoring up could forestall, and the administration had been trapped by the slow but irrevocable cave-in that occurred after Capp and his unit had been apprehended for the Gateway Trust break-in.

There had been three carpenter units, each unaware of the others. And the only unit the public had become aware of was Capp's. The press, the Senate Investigative Committee, the prosecution, had no idea of the magnitude of the iceberg beneath the tip with which they'd dealt. Or if they did have an idea, they chose not to pursue it, conveniently considering the matter closed after Berwin's resignation. Perralt's unit had been engaged in activities that would have made Gateway seem trivial.

Chereno knew now that Perralt was in Colorado at the time of Victor Wezenski's murder. And when Haggar had died in Kentucky, Perralt was in Chicago on business.

Chereno had placed almost everyone on his list elsewhere at the times of at least two of the murders. All but three men: Wilson Capp, Raul Esteben and Julian Zayas. Chereno knew how loyal the two Cubans were to Capp. And of course there was the matter of Raul Esteben being killed on the same day in the same vicinity as Haggar's death. The evidence, circumstantial though it was, left little doubt.

Chereno was sure now he was looking for Wilson Capp.

Capp was by far the most formidable quarry on Chereno's list of suspects. Chereno was aware of Capp's record, the dangerous work in Berlin, the Martindale coup, the death duel in the Paris elevator with the would-be assassin of de Gaulle, the brief but brilliant work in Saigon. The Gateway foul-up had hardly been Capp's fault. A passerby, trespassing to corner his runaway German shepherd, had noticed signs of entry at the bank and raised an alarm. In the United States, in peacetime, there was no way to silence him. It was to Capp's credit that all but one man had escaped with what they had come to obtain.

"It's hopeless," Al, Tuffy's handler, said suddenly and with finality. Chereno watched him reach into a leather case and withdraw a large hypodermic syringe. Al gave the dog a shot of a milky pink substance, then wiped the needle on the leg of his bib overalls and replaced it in the case. Within seconds Tuffy's quivering flank was still.

"Too bad," a voice said, and Chereno looked up to see that DeMet, Zeb's handler, had walked up behind him. "You could have used him for stud."

"He fought longer than he should have," Al said, folding the blanket over the dog's body.

"If we could find such a heart in a man, eh?" DeMet said.

Tuffy's handler nodded. Chereno moved away.

People were walking out of the barn now. Either the fights were ended or there was to be an intermission. The woman with the heavily jeweled necklace was walking beside a small man wearing a turquoise-beaded shirt and polished black boots. Several people were walking across the grass toward Al and DeMet to console, congratulate and talk about the fight and the merits of each dog.

Chereno walked along the row of cars to where his Dodge was parked. The car was no longer in the shade, and reflected in the sun-glazed window was the determined but apprehensive image of the approaching Chereno. Chereno jerked the car door open to escape the image and got in.

He started the Dodge and backed it out onto leveler ground, then turned hard left and drove toward the rough dirt road that was the only route to or from the secluded old barn. The steering wheel began to dance in his hands, signaling with scientific accuracy the location of each irregularity in the road.

As he drove, Chereno chewed the blade of grass that was still wedged in his teeth. He thought about the dog Tuffy, worn and mutilated, compelled by burning, unrelenting instinct to continue his fight.

"If we could find such a heart in a man . . ." DeMet had said wistfully.

He had never met Wilson Capp.

☒ 26

CAPP LAY IN BED with his eyes open. Next to him Myra lay on her side, facing him, her knees drawn up and her arms crooked beneath her wadded pillow. The bedroom was suspended between soft light and soft shadow, darkness and dawn. An oval of light on the wall, a reflection from Myra's vanity mirror, was slowly merging with the pale-yellow tone of the bedroom and would soon disappear.

The illuminated clock on the table near Capp was making a low electrical gurgling sound. Outside, the owl that lived in the walnut tree hooted three times, then was quiet. Capp knew that Myra was awake beside him.

He had given his deepening circumstances a great deal of thought, and he was sure Myra knew he was involved in the Gateway deaths. Of course she'd said nothing about the subject, and they'd continued to communicate in the habitual circumventing language peculiar to their marriage.

Myra had no way of knowing the unspoken thing between them had been changed. No longer was it only the plodding machinery of the law threatening Capp. Now a much more imaginative and intrepid pursuer was part of the picture, someone no doubt cut from the same cloth as Capp. A killer had been set to catch a killer. The game was narrowing to the experts.

Downstairs the automatic coffee brewer had turned itself on, and the brightening bedroom was permeated by the morning scent of fresh coffee. The oval of light on the wall had disappeared.

Capp said, "I'm going to be away for some time."

From beside him Myra's voice was compliant and trusting, and somewhat resigned. "All right."

"The deaths of the Gateway people, they're more than coincidence."

"I was sure they were," she said, as if they were discussing the plot of a movie they'd just seen. Perhaps that was how she looked at things, maintained her sanity-saving detachment.

"We should face the fact that I might be on the killer's list of future victims," Capp said. "I'm going to drop out of sight for a while."

Myra lay silently, in the same languid fetal position.

"I want you to be safe while I'm gone," Capp told her.

"I'll stay here. There really isn't any reason to think I might be in danger."

At first her reply startled Capp, then he realized she meant that none of the other Gateway wives had so far figured in the series of murders.

"You're right," he said. "I think you should be okay here."

Myra stirred, threw back the cover, then stood up slowly as if to let gravity shed the smooth residue of sleep from her. She stretched with an inhibited sideways thrust of her arms, walked to the closet door and put on her robe.

"Coffee?" she asked, pulling the robe's long sash belt tight.

Capp nodded and watched her walk from the bedroom. He heard the faint slapping pad of her soft slippers as she descended the carpeted stairs to the kitchen.

He propped his pillow against the headboard for support and sat up in bed. But for the occasional sounds of Myra below in the kitchen, the morning was silent.

Capp knew that Myra didn't believe what he had told her, but she accepted it. Somehow she was able to reconcile herself to that distinction.

Myra returned to the bedroom carrying two cups of coffee.

The morning newspaper was tucked beneath her arm. She handed Capp his coffee and extended her right elbow to let the paper drop near him.

Careful not to spill his steaming coffee, Capp sat up straighter against his propped pillow.

Myra automatically flicked on the TV set as she walked past it, carrying her cup to her vanity. After a few sips of coffee, she set the cup on the vanity's glass top, opened a drawer and began sorting through a tangle of panty hose.

The national weather forecast segment of the morning news was on the TV. Capp ignored it and turned his attention to the newspaper.

On the front page were a few juicy quotes from a taped television interview of Andrew Berwin that had aired the previous night. Interviewing Berwin was Harold Fein, the English journalist and entertainment personality. It was like Berwin to give his series of exclusive interviews to a foreign correspondent. Capp read with interest:

"'I maintain that I behaved properly,' says Berwin in historic Fein interview. States impeachment proceedings would have found him blameless but that country would have been subjected to severe governmental crisis at worst possible time."

On page 4-D the paper carried the entire verbatim account of the interview.

Myra was in the bathroom now. Capp could hear water thundering into the tub for her bath. He spread the pages of the newspaper and turned them with much crinkling to 4-D.

Berwin's answers to Fein's sometimes probing questions were predictable. He feigned total lack of knowledge about many of the objectionable activities that had occurred during his presidency. Yet he defended these activities as necessary, indeed vital, to the well-being of the nation. History, he was sure, would regard him in a much more favorable light than did his contemporaries, whose views had been shaped by a malicious, unknowledgeable news media. And yes, a president should be free to interpret the law with a sometimes necessary speed toward good purpose that it was impossible for the courts to provide. If some chose to regard that as being "above the law," let them.

But it was an obscure area of the interview that most caught Capp's attention:

> *Fein:* After the pace of your life as president, do you sometimes find it unbearably lonely here at Lost Palms?
>
> *Berwin:* Oh, sometimes it's lonely, as if I'm waiting in Bethany, but I keep busy with my correspondence and personal matters. It isn't as if I'm forgotten, or you wouldn't be here interviewing me, would you?
>
> *Fein:* You say you're not forgotten, sir, but in what way do you believe you're remembered? . . .

It seemed to Capp that Harold Fein hadn't picked up on the salient point, possibly because Fein was Jewish. Or because Berwin was fond of referring to or quoting from the Bible. Or perhaps what Berwin had said could mean something to the man who had stood over the dying Mark Haggar, the man Haggar had in his final, failing moments mistaken for a priest.

Capp remembered it easily from his rigid midwestern upbringing, from that most fascinating and awe-inspiring lesson of his Bible school days.

Bethany was the city wherein Jesus had raised up Lazarus from the dead.

And dying in Kentucky, seeking a priest's forgiveness for his sins, Mark Haggar's last word had been "Lazarus."

That Haggar would at the instant of his death coincidentally refer to a biblical subject that Berwin would later allude to during a TV interview seemed highly unlikely.

Had Berwin mentioned Bethany deliberately as a secret gesture of contempt for the press? Or had he subconsciously let slip something potentially harmful in a manifestation of the "death wish" many of his detractors claimed had led to his political destruction? Or did the dual reference, even under such extraordinary circumstances, mean nothing at all?

Capp realized that he'd been straining forward as he read. His neck was stiff and sore. He laid the paper aside and let his head sink back into the pillow. Staring up at the ceiling, he let out a soft, incredulous laugh, glad that Myra was still running her bath water and couldn't hear him.

Lazarus . . . It might mean nothing, or it might mean something astounding in its audacity.

☒ 27

THE DOORBELL HAD CHIMED five times. Myra turned on the front porch light, opened the door with some agitation and stared out at the man standing smiling on the front porch.

He flashed identification with practiced nonchalance and returned his wallet to an inside pocket of his gray suitcoat.

"My name is Clyde Hawker, Mrs. Capp. I'm with the FBI. Mr. Capp in?"

"No," Myra said, which was true. Capp had left as planned that afternoon.

Hawker's smile continued to radiate good humor. He seemed oblivious to the circling moths attracted by the porch light, flitting in quick, shadowed darts about his face. He was aware that some of the moths were getting inside the house, and that Myra didn't like that.

"May I come in?" he asked.

Myra stepped aside to let him enter, turned off the porch light and closed the door.

"If your husband isn't home, I'd like to ask you a few questions," Hawker said.

"May I see your identification again?"

Hawker nodded, understanding, and fished in his pocket for his leather wallet.

Myra studied the identification carefully. It appeared genuine, but she knew that didn't necessarily mean that it was. It did mean that if Hawker wasn't a bona fide FBI agent he was a pro with competent people behind him. She handed back the identification and invited him into the living room.

"A very nice home," he commented, glancing around with what seemed to be admiration.

"Please sit down."

He chose the daintiest chair in the room, so that his bulk would be all the more intimidating. "Do you mind?" he asked, holding up a pack of cigarettes. Myra said that she didn't and he touched the flame of a thin gold lighter to tobacco. "Now," he said, exhaling a lungful of smoke, "where is your husband, Mrs. Capp?"

"I don't know."

"How long has he been gone?"

"Since early this afternoon." Myra spoke the truth without hesitation.

"And you have no way of reaching him?"

"No . . . no way of reaching him."

The smile, quite beautiful. "That doesn't strike me as unusual, Mrs. Capp. Your husband and I are in much the same business. I'm a widower, but when Clarice was alive I seldom told her anything it might be dangerous for her to know."

Myra was standing near the mantel, her hands before her and her fingers loosely knitted. "I doubt that any danger would be involved, Mr. Hawker. Wilson's work has simply made him habitually secretive. And I suppose with good reason."

"Believe it, Mrs. Capp, believe it." He looked at her and chuckled softly. "So many books are written about the exploits of spies and government agents. It's the wives who really deserve the praise."

"Oh, not entirely." What was he getting at?

"If I were your husband, Mrs. Capp, I'd be a bit concerned for my safety. I mean, with this series of Gateway deaths. Has he ever talked to you about the possibility that he might be on the killer's list?" He stroked his chin. "Or of you being on it?"

"Weren't some of the deaths accidental?"

"Well, we don't know for sure. I'm speculating, putting myself in your husband's place. If I were him, I'd be uneasy."

"Of course Wilson is uneasy at times."

"Is that why he's disappeared this time?"

"It could be. I don't know. Would you blame him?"

"Not at all. It's the smart move to make. What has he said to you about the Gateway deaths?"

"I don't recall, really," Myra replied. "The sort of things you'd expect from reading the newspapers."

"Did he discern a pattern in the deaths?"

"He was like you, Mr. Hawker. He could only speculate."

Hawker drew on his cigarette, seemed to examine the smoke as he exhaled. "So much for speculation . . ."

"I'm sorry I can't help you."

"And I'm sorry I can't help you, Mrs. Capp." Hawker delivered this standard line with the throwaway ease born of long experience. He stood and flicked cigarette ash into a brass ashtray. "If Mr. Capp gets in touch, would you call this number?" He laid a small white business card, engraved with only a phone number, alongside the ashtray. "Perhaps we could furnish him some protection if he's truly concerned."

"I'll be glad to phone you," Myra said, seeing Hawker to the door. "And I'll tell my husband you were by."

"I appreciate that, you can be sure." He gave her his beatific smile as he left.

Hawker sat in his car for some time in front of the Capp home. He was sure Myra Capp would be watching to see when he'd drive away. It couldn't hurt to let her do some of her own speculation.

Hawker turned on the car radio and punched buttons in an attempt to get some relaxing music. He encountered only news and hard rock. Giving up, he settled for a sportscaster's account of a major league baseball manager unexpectedly being fired. The sportscaster opined that there was a high mortality rate in that business.

When a singing commercial for denture cream came over the speaker, Hawker decided that he'd sat long enough in front of the house. He was sure Myra Capp was telling the truth about not knowing Capp's whereabouts, and if Capp was as thorough a professional as his record indicated, she would never know until he chose to tell her.

"You can even eat apples!" the announcer assured Hawker from the dashboard speaker. Hawker started the car and drove away.

☒ 28

CAPP AND JULIAN STOOD on Fourth Street looking across the busy avenue at the twenty-story apartment building where David Wellman lived. Financially, Wellman had not done as well as many of the Gateway principals; the apartment building, in a declining neighborhood in New York, bore a tarnished brass plaque pretentiously labeled the Belmont Towers. An old, weathered building with stone facing that went up three stories, it displayed an entranceway adorned with chipped and disfigured stone sea nymphs. Someone had used red crayon to equip one of the sea nymphs with oversized, unsymmetrical nipples. Beneath the Belmont Towers was a parking lot with private spaces for the tenants and driveways onto Fourth Street and St. Charles Street.

Julian crossed the street and entered the Belmont Towers first.

Ten minutes later Capp crossed the street and walked past the sea nymphs into the high-ceilinged, paneled lobby. He let the wood-framed glass door swing shut noisily and crossed the lobby to the elevators.

After pushing the up button he glanced about. He was alone. The pale marble floor was scuffed and littered with extinguished cigarette butts that had left tiny blackened spots. The only sound was the singing and clacking of the elevator cables. An ornate black arrow above the closed elevator doors progressed jerkily past the midway numeral *10* and began the spasmodic descent to *L*. Capp noticed that the other elevator also was descending but had stopped at the fourteenth floor.

When the elevator arrived and the doors hissed open, a dark-haired woman carrying a trembling white poodle stepped out and walked past Capp without glancing at him. Capp entered the elevator and pressed the *17* button.

At the end of a curved, carpeted hall on the seventeenth floor was apartment 17-E, where David Wellman lived.

But Wellman wasn't home. Julian had let himself in with a burglar's ease, and when Capp knocked once lightly on 17-E's door it opened immediately. Capp stepped inside and Julian closed the door behind him.

The apartment was small and almost military-neat, furnished with expensive contemporary furniture that was left over from Wellman's more affluent days. Above a writing desk against one wall hung a large framed aerial view of Washington, D.C., with the White House slightly left of center. Picasso prints adorned the opposite wall, arranged symmetrically above a long striped sofa. To the left of the sofa, angled in the corner, was a tall bookcase packed with books, most of which were paperbacks. Capp could see into the bedroom, which was as tidy as the living room, and he could see the sink and a corner of a copper-toned refrigerator in the small kitchen. Someone in an apartment above ran water and the sound was picked up faintly in the kitchen pipes like a discontented sigh.

Capp considered searching the apartment, but there was no guarantee as to the exact time Wellman would arrive home. And once Wellman got there, things would have to go smoothly, without wasted time and without disorder that needed to be set straight.

Julian sat down calmly on the sofa, seemingly relaxed but with his senses tuned for the sound of Wellman's key in the lock. Capp did go to the desk and idly examine its contents. He found only the expected canceled checks, household bills, bank statements, receipts, a few uninteresting personal letters.

He turned away from the desk and went to the window to look down onto Fourth Street, more for something to do than to watch for Wellman. Capp was sure Wellman would park in the basement garage and take the elevator.

Wind rattled the windowpane and a few large drops of rain smacked against the glass. Lights were being turned on in the building across the street. Capp pulled the drapes closed, leaving Wellman's living room softly lighted by the illumination that filtered in through the doorways to kitchen and bedroom. Rectangles of light from each doorway lay on the gold shag carpet.

Julian stood suddenly at the scratch of metal on metal.

By the time the ratchety penetration of Wellman's key in the lock sounded, Capp and Julian were standing over by the sofa, out of sight of the doorway. They heard Wellman enter, close and relock the door.

He was slipping his keys into his pants pocket as he walked past the two intruders without seeing them, toward the kitchen, carrying a small grocery bag beneath his left arm.

"Wellman," Capp said softly.

Wellman stiffened, his back arched as if he'd been struck. The bag dropped, split with a brief tearing sound, and a red and white soup can rolled a foot or two on the thick carpet.

When Wellman turned toward them his face was white, his mouth distorted by fear and struggling to shape words. He'd lost a good deal of his mottled gray hair, Capp noticed, and his apple-cheeked yet serious face had aged. He looked very much like an old and decadent Cupid.

"Holy Christ! . . ." he managed to stammer at last. A fleck of saliva clung to his chin.

"Sit down," Capp told him. Capp and Julian stepped forward so they stood on either side of Wellman, and Wellman went to the sofa and sat. Capp and Julian remained standing.

Capp switched on a tall table lamp. The sudden brilliance seemed to startle Wellman as he squinted up at Capp, then let his narrowed eyes dart to Julian. Capp waited for Wellman to recover from his shock.

Wellman's hands were trembling but he was breathing deeply and steadily. "What do you want?" he asked Capp in a wheezing tone of fear. There were white splotches at the corners of his mouth.

Capp didn't answer.

"You . . ." Wellman said. "You killed the others . . ."

"We want to know about Lazarus," Capp said.

"Lazarus?"

Julian held out a new single-edged razor blade beneath the light from the table lamp. Yellow brightness played over precision-honed steel.

"My friend is an expert with that," Capp said. "You'll recognize the technique from the French *Sureté* during the war. He'll slit the flesh beneath one of your fingernails so that the nail can easily be bent back, enlarging and tearing the cut until you choose to talk. Or you can remain silent and look forward to nine more fingernails. Then your toes."

Wellman was perspiring and his lips moved soundlessly as he stared at the blade held steady in Julian's manicured hand. He was arriving at the horrifying realization that Capp and Julian were serious.

"Lazarus," Capp reminded him.

Wellman nodded.

Julian smiled.

"I don't know everything," Wellman said, "but I'll tell you what I do know." He began to squirm in the sofa corner as if some agonizing current were running through him. "It started years ago, with the White House Enemies List. It was Stauker who composed the list, who was in charge of researching for it. While doing his investigative work, he came across some interesting information about a junior senator. The man wasn't placed on the Enemies List, but Stauker shared his information with Berwin."

Julian was using the razor blade to trim the cuticle on his left thumb.

"Which information was?" Capp asked.

"The senator had had a previous marriage," Wellman continued hastily. "No one seemed to know about it outside of a few people in the small town where he came from. It had happened long ago, when he was eighteen and his bride was seventeen. Within a month after the marriage the bride died in a fall down some stairs. A doctor who was a family friend, now dead, performed the autopsy on the girl and faked the death certificate. Stauker somehow got something on the doctor, who was an old man and terminally ill, and got his statement on tape."

"What do you mean by 'faked the death certificate'?"

"The girl was murdered. An exhumation of her body would prove that her skull wounds were inconsistent with a fall. That fact, along with the doctor's taped testimony, would open a homicide case with the husband as prime suspect. It would topple a lot of dominoes."

"So the senator is being blackmailed."

"In a sense. Berwin owns him, has had him by the short hairs for years."

"So how is this information being used?"

"For Lazarus. The senator is now a presidential candidate, and Berwin and a select few are backing him."

Capp said nothing. Julian laughed and cursed vehemently in Spanish. In the following silence, more wind-driven raindrops splattered loudly against the window.

"The bag of tricks is open again," Wellman said, "anonymous letters, planted news items, leaked information, phony endorsements, hidden contributions. Only it's all being done more carefully this time around, even though it's safer. We've learned where not to go wrong. And the public is actually less aware now than they were before Gateway; they're sated, and they're lulled by the misconception that everyone in Washington has turned over a new leaf and there are watchdogs everywhere. It makes it all easier for us. And now we've got nothing to lose and everything to gain. They've put us in that position."

Wellman sat back, almost relaxed now. He seemed oddly relieved at having released his information to Capp. It was as if he thought that Capp would understand why such actions were justified and so would forgive him. Men afraid for their lives seek absolution where they can find it.

Capp turned away from Wellman and paced to the closed drapes and the faint sound of wind rushing by outside like a swift river. He realized now why things had become complicated. He had stepped in shit of the worst kind.

He turned suddenly and looked at Wellman. Julian was very still.

"Berwin will do whatever's necessary for his man to be elected," Wellman said.

Capp walked back to stand near him. "Who is the candidate?"

"I don't know."

"Why is he being backed?"

"I don't know that, either."

Julian said, "He's out of his fucking mind."

"I swear to *God,* I don't know!" Wellman was squirming again, like a small boy who'd put off going to the bathroom. "Only a select few know that. For security! Christ, you must understand that! You must know I'm telling the truth!"

Capp was reasonably sure that Wellman was telling all he knew. It was like Berwin to keep any circle of knowledge as tight as possible. And to create enough smoke so that someone in Wellman's position wouldn't be able to learn anything through process of elimination.

"Give me a guess as to which candidate," Capp said.

"It would be an uneducated guess, no better than yours. I honestly have no idea." Wellman was clutching the material of his pants legs to keep his hands steady, squeezing so hard that his knuckles were whitened and one fingernail was visibly sunk into the flesh of his palm. "Why would I lie to you? You're here to kill me anyway, aren't you? You killed the others . . ." He lowered his head and tensed his body as if anticipating a blow.

"You're the one who says we killed the others," Capp told him. "All we want is information. But it has to be straight and complete."

Wellman's voice was low, resigned. "I've given it to you as straight and complete as I know how."

Capp nodded to Julian, who moved his hand inside his shirt for the knotted rope wrapped about his waist.

Wellman jerked his head up and started to say something, but the door buzzer rasped three times like a gigantic marauding insect in the kitchen.

Julian removed his hand from inside his shirt and fastened the button.

Wellman bolted from the sofa before Capp or Julian could move. He was at the front door by the time each of them had taken a step toward him. Then the door was open and a slender, middle-aged woman wearing slacks and a flowered blouse peered in from behind round, fashionably oversized glasses.

She could only perceive Capp and Julian as shadowed figures. She squinted through her glasses at Wellman.

"Are you all right, Mr. Wellman?"

"Of course, Adelle. Come in, please." Wellman had never sounded that happy to see anyone. "These are friends of mine. They just stood up to leave."

Adelle stepped inside, lifting one long leg over the threshold as if stepping into water. She was carrying a small notebook and a large manila envelope.

"I saw you come home," she told Wellman. "I've been waiting for you. It's about the money for Mrs. Charlath's wreath. Her husband's funeral's day after tomorrow."

"I'm glad you caught me in," Wellman said. He reached for his wallet and withdrew a bill, but he didn't hand the money to Adelle. "Mrs. Charlath's a woman on the fourth floor," he explained to Capp and Julian. "Her husband died of cancer yesterday." He stood staring at them, moving aside as if making room for them to leave before he handed Adelle the wreath money.

"Let's hope they find a cure before long," Capp said. He nodded to Wellman and Adelle and left the apartment quickly with Julian behind him.

"Amen," Adelle said behind them, as they walked toward the elevators.

Capp heard the sound of Wellman's apartment door closing.

Inside the descending elevator, Capp and Julian glanced at each other. Julian seemed faintly worried.

"Do you think he'll call the police?" he asked Capp.

"He can't. Not without blowing the whistle on Lazarus. The only people who are going to hear about our visit are those involved with Lazarus, including our friend who's been dogging us lately."

"Do you think we should go back?"

"No," Capp said. "Wellman will be on the phone behind locked doors two seconds after his neighbor leaves with her wreath money." His voice was laden with contempt.

The elevator stopped for a man and woman on the ninth floor, and Capp and Julian were silent the rest of the way down.

Outside, the drizzle had stopped but the wind was a steady force. Capp told Julian that he would sort things out, then phone him at his motel. They had arrived in separate cars, parked in opposite directions from the Belmont Towers.

As Capp walked toward where his car was parked, he turned up the collar of his sport coat. He hadn't brought his all-weather coat, and the wind was suddenly damp and cold on the back of his neck.

It disturbed him in a subtly unsettling way that he and

Julian had been interrupted in such a manner in Wellman's apartment. A collection for a funeral wreath! It was almost as if Death had intervened to save Wellman for another time.

Capp snorted at the absurdity of his thoughts. He had never been superstitious, and it was too late in life to change.

☒ 29

"I'm convinced I'm alive because of luck," David Wellman said. "They had every intention of killing me."

"Then really there was no point in telling them about Lazarus," Alex Whitencroft said.

"Bullshit," Wellman told him. He didn't know if Whitencroft was serious. "You know they could have made me or anyone else talk."

"That fingernail thing is effective," Whitencroft agreed.

The conversation was taking place in Whitencroft's fortieth-floor luxury apartment that featured a balcony view of Central Park. In the next room were two private bodyguards loyal to and assigned by Chereno. The apartment was expertly wired with a sensitive alarm system.

"It's obvious that you don't minimize any danger to yourself," Wellman said acidly, remembering the bodyguards. He took another sip of the scotch and seltzer Whitencroft had given him.

"I begin my prison term in less than a week," Whitencroft said. "Until then I've decided to make myself a virtual prisoner here, for personal security." He walked to the wide sliding glass doors that led to the balcony and looked out over the green trees and winding avenues below. "And it's quite secure here, though God knows what goes on down there in the park."

Whitencroft was a large man, obese but with long limbs. Framed in the square of light from the balcony, he appeared grotesquely spidery. He drew a long-stemmed pipe from his side pocket and began packing it with tobacco. A pipe was his favorite prop. Like many pipe smokers, when confused or pressed for that which he couldn't deliver, he played for time behind the ritualistic paraphernalia of his habit. It was from Whitencroft that Haggar had learned the tactical advantages of the pipe smoker.

"I long suspected it was Capp working his way up the ladder in revenge," Whitencroft said. "He's the sort who might picture himself as a wronged idealist in a world of pure reason."

Wellman paced back and forth over plush cream-colored carpet. "After last night, I don't take him lightly. I want protection."

Whitencroft drew on his pipe stem, staring at the glowing bowl with a faintly cross-eyed expression of concern. "Understandable."

"Will you talk to Berwin for me?"

"Of course. But have you considered simply going into hiding temporarily?"

"Like Mark Haggar?"

Whitencroft sucked noisily on the pipe stem and nodded his understanding of Wellman's point of view, the folds of flesh that swelled over his white collar seeming to expand and contract like a bellows.

Wellman stopped pacing and worked on his scotch and seltzer. He was aware that if he knew the identity of the Lazarus candidate and the intricacies of the plan as Whitencroft did, there would be no need to come begging for protection. Whitencroft would be safe, here and in prison. And after the election in November, his prison stay figured to be brief.

"I think you should know," Whitencroft said, "that we have someone working on this, have had for some time."

"Someone tracking Capp?"

"Not Capp specifically. We couldn't be sure who we were looking for until now. But now the search can be focused full strength on Capp. The situation will soon resolve itself."

The "will soon resolve itself" stance had long been one of Whitencroft's favorite ways of telling his people he would do nothing to change the status quo. It had once prompted one of his harried aides—long since banished—to shout at him in anger to "go resolve yourself!" Wellman wondered what the aide was doing now.

"We both know Capp personally," Wellman said. "He's more than an idealist, he's a fanatic. He won't stop. He'll have to be stopped."

"Yes, it's reached a point where he has little choice but to continue to an unfortunate conclusion." With the balanced grace characteristic of certain fat men, Whitencroft lowered his bulk into a tufted beige chair. He tapped the underside of his pipe bowl into the palm of his left hand. "I'll send Martin, one of my bodyguards, to escort you home," he said to Wellman. "Then I suggest you lock yourself in and if you must leave see to it that you're surrounded by as many people as possible. I don't see it as likely that Capp will try anything again soon at your apartment, but try to stay there and stay alert. Do you have a firearm?"

"No."

Whitencroft seemed to have slipped back twenty years, to when he was ACTIVE's deputy director. "Go to a sporting goods store and purchase a cheap single-shot twelve-gauge shotgun. There's no need for a permit for that. Keep it handy at home; especially have it near you at night, just beneath the bed where you can reach it. And sound-rig your apartment with strings and metal cooking utensils."

"I know all those time-worn precautions," Wellman said. "Capp knows them too."

Whitencroft told him, "Crude as they are, they are not easily circumvented. I'll speak to Berwin when I make my regular contact, then phone you tomorrow."

Wellman finished his drink, aware that it was time to leave. "Thanks, Alex. I know you'll do what you can." Fear haunted the inflections of his voice.

Whitencroft went with him into the next room, where the two bodyguards were ensconced. One was seated with his eyes partly closed, as if daydreaming, but there was a heavy-lidded, lizardlike alertness to his glance as Whitencroft and Wellman entered the room. The other bodyguard was standing, drinking from a Coca-Cola can. Both men were of average height but bulky beneath their dark suits. They were of Latin descent, Wellman noted. Probably Cuban expatriates. The seated man seemed vaguely familiar.

"Martin," Whitencroft said to the seated man. "I'd like you to escort Mr. Wellman to his apartment, then return here."

Martin stood up slowly and buttoned his suit coat. He was wearing a multicolored violently striped tie. Martin had worked with Chereno's carpenter unit during the administration, and had worked for Chereno off and on since. He was devoted to Chereno, and Chereno had told him to follow Whitencroft's instructions.

"I'll be in touch," Whitencroft reassured Wellman.

Wellman nodded and left with Martin.

When Wellman had gone, Whitencroft went into his study and closed the door. It would be impossible to speak to Berwin until the prearranged report time in six hours. Whitencroft slid his weight into the chair behind the desk, then grunted with the slight effort of reaching for the telephone and pulling it toward him. He dialed Dwayne Stauker's number and switched on the long neon desk lamp. A neon tube burning nearby would disrupt any planted microtransmitter.

"This is Wit," Whitencroft said, when Stauker had answered the phone. "Something's come up concerning the hunt."

"No need to talk gibberish, Alex," Stauker said in his sardonic urbane voice. "A scrambler's been placed on your phone."

"Wellman was here. He told me that Wilson Capp paid

him a visit last night and questioned him about Lazarus. He was sure Capp and a slender, handsome Cuban were about to kill him when a neighbor interrupted and Wellman finessed them out."

"What did Wellman tell them about Lazarus?"

"What he knew," Whitencroft replied.

Stauker was silent. "Did Capp let slip how he found out there was a Lazarus?" he finally asked.

"Capp doesn't let slip anything," Whitencroft said.

"Where's Wellman now?"

"I sent him home with Martin, told him to lock himself in and not go out unless he had to."

"Is he rattled?"

"Yes, but he'll hold."

"The man with Capp would be Julian Zayas," Stauker said.

Whitencroft was familiar with the name and immediately recalled the face. Zayas had been one of the Gateway carpenters who had been convicted and served his time.

"I'll speak with the Man," Stauker said, and hung up abruptly.

Whitencroft slipped the perspiration-damp receiver into its cradle, remained seated and relighted his pipe. He dropped the stunted black remains of the burnt match into an ashtray. In the smoke-hazed quiet of his study he recalled past dangerous days and a precautionary maxim that he hadn't thought of in years: When the shit hits the fan, pull the plug.

But of course there was no other way to deal with Wilson Capp.

☒ 30

Hawker stood in a doorway across the street from Peterson's Pawnshop and waited for Peterson to be alone. A slight, frightened-looking man in a white jacket had been inside the shop talking to Peterson for the past half hour. Probably discussing the sale of stolen merchandise, Hawker thought, but he wasn't interested in Peterson's possible nefarious sidelines.

Finally the man in the white jacket left, carrying a small brown paper bag he hadn't had when he entered. He was whistling.

Hawker looked both ways, then crossed the street toward the tiny shop with its merchandise-laden show window. A bell above the door jingled as he went inside.

Peterson was a small, frowning man with an aura of anger about his dark features. His expression seemed to say, "The world is a bitch but I cope with it as best I can." Probably that was exactly how he felt. He looked expectantly at Hawker and sniffed loudly.

"A cold?" Hawker asked, smiling.

Peterson shook his head. "Some kinda damn allergy. You buying or selling?"

"Neither," Hawker said. "I need to ask you some questions about your brother-in-law, Julian Zayas."

"You're cops, aren't you?"

"No. I just need to find Julian and talk with him."

Peterson laughed and shrugged. "Well, you come to the wrong place. We don't get on real well, Julian and me. How come you need to talk with him?"

"Tell you the truth, he owes me money."

"Then we oughta cry on each other's shoulders. He owes me money, too." Peterson's whining tone left little doubt that he was one of the world's most frequent victims.

"Do you know where he can be reached?"

Peterson shook his head no, scratched violently with a knuckle behind his left ear. "Did you try Shirley?"

"His wife?"

"Yeah, and tough luck for her. The stupid bitch."

"She's your sister, isn't she?"

"Right. I got the brains and she got the looks. Neither of us got any luck." Peterson's face was a mask of pure misery.

"Well, one thing she doesn't know is where Julian is."

"I'm not surprised. And if he doesn't let his wife know where he's at for the past three weeks, he's not likely to fill me in on what he's been doing."

"She hasn't heard from him in three weeks?"

"At least. Except maybe he's phoned a few times. He's an odd duck. If I were you I'd do what I did about the money he owes."

"What's that?"

"Forget it," Peterson said. "I mean, don't try to lean on him —not in any way at all. You don't want to get Julian mad, because you can't tell when he's mad. He just gets his evens. I'd forget the debt. If he decides to pay you, you're lucky."

The bell above the door jangled behind Hawker.

"How about phoning this number if you do find out where he's at," Hawker said, laying his card on the counter. "Maybe, in a diplomatic way, I can arrange it so he pays both of us."

Now Peterson looked worried. "I wouldn't want you to . . . you know . . ."

"Get rough?"

"Right."

Hawker smiled. "Don't worry. The last thing I want to do is see your brother-in-law hurt."

"I was worried," Peterson said, "but not about Julian."

He looked beyond Hawker at the customer who'd entered the shop. He seemed aggravated and suspicious. "Help you?"

"Thanks, Mr. Peterson," Hawker said, and walked back out onto the sidewalk to leave Peterson and an old man with a clarinet to haggle in private.

Hawker was getting nowhere, sifting meticulously and finding nothing. Of course, things often had a way of happening all at once.

It was almost noon and starting to warm up. Hawker had some hours to spare, so he went into a cool hotel lounge and sat at the bar drinking a cold beer. He thought best in such a relaxing setting.

There was one particularly interesting aspect of the case. There were only so many potential victims. Each time the murderer killed, he was narrowing the scope of his future activities. So with each success, the murderer moved closer to being apprehended; ultimately success would translate into failure.

Hawker reflected over his icy beer that that was generally the way of the world.

Peterson knew.

☒ 31

WHITENCROFT WAS PERSPIRING as only a fat man can.

The air-conditioning unit five stories above him on the roof had broken down the night before, and the repairmen were just now getting around to fixing it.

Sipping his fourth gin and tonic, Whitencroft slumped on the sofa and wondered how cool it would be in prison. Wouldn't the press be shocked if he showed up early to begin his sentence? Or was the press beyond shock?

Whitencroft had talked with Berwin after calling Stauker. He'd learned very little. Which meant there'd been little to relay to Wellman except Berwin's reassurances. Berwin and Stauker were to meet this evening.

The temperature in the apartment was 86 by the desk thermometer. Whitencroft was glad he didn't have a hygrometer to let him know the humidity. The air was syrupy with the dampness of one of those almost maliciously hot cloudless days. Already Con Edison was threatening brownouts.

The white short-sleeved polo shirt Whitencroft wore clung to the folds of his torso, bunched uncomfortably beneath his arms. It embarrassed him somewhat to notice that the only concession to the heat his bodyguards had made was to remove their suit coats. Ties were intact. Whitencroft glanced down at the tiny green alligator embroidered above his shirt pocket and decided that it should feel right at home.

A rivulet of sweat zigzagged like a demented insect down Whitencroft's arm. He took a long sip of his drink, then pushed himself up from the sofa and plodded to the phone.

For the fifth time that day he dialed management's number and complained about the delay in repairing the air-conditioning unit. For the fifth time it got him nowhere.

He returned to the sofa and sat down. He reached for his pipe, then changed his mind. It was too hot even to smoke. He stood up again, walked agitatedly to the bookcase for something to read that would take his mind off the heat. His eyes seemed to fasten only on the most discomfiting titles, from *Dante's Inferno* to Ball's *In the Heat of the Night.*

Whitencroft longed for the night: if the sun went down the temperature would drop with it.

Earlier, accompanied by his bodyguards, Whitencroft had gone to an air-conditioned restaurant. But he'd been unable to relax. He couldn't escape a sense of impending danger as he sat picking at an omelet-and-pancakes brunch, watching those people who'd seemed to pay an undue amount of attention to him, starting at the ringing clatter of a dropped tray of silverware. He'd decided to do the intelligent if uncomfortable thing and return to the apartment.

That had been before noon, when it was cooler.

Whitencroft walked to the bar and mixed himself another gin and tonic, this time running the ice cubes through an electric crusher so the drink would be instantly cold even if slightly diluted.

He downed almost half of it in one long, luxurious sip. If he was beginning to feel the effects of the liquor, good; that would make the heat somewhat less torturous.

Through the glass door to his private balcony, Whitencroft saw the nylon webbing of the chaise longue quiver. At least there was a slight breeze out there. Carrying his drink, he slid open the door and stepped outside.

The balcony was in shade and seemed cooler than it actually was. A faint breeze played over Whitencroft's soaked, plastered shirt and brought some small relief from the heat. He sipped his drink and turned his body to take in the green view of the park far below. Two pigeons, one of them completely white, flapped up toward him, then passed out of sight as they found a place to perch several stories down. Whitencroft began chewing noisily on a mouthful of crushed ice and turned to gaze in the opposite direction.

The high-velocity soft-tipped bullet struck him squarely in the chest. The bullet split as it shattered the thick breastbone, half of it veering upward to lodge in the pharynx, the other half tumbling as it ripped through the left auricle of the heart and tore a large exit wound in Whitencroft's back.

The sliding glass door behind him was shatterproof: it turned milk-white patterned by opaque red swirls that would have made an interesting Rorschach test.

Whitencroft staggered two incredulous steps on thick, rubberized legs. Life drained visibly from him.

He was dead when he toppled over the balcony railing, to fall limply, like an oversized Hollywood dummy, to the avenue below.

☒ 32

"I DIDN'T EXPECT YOU to come back here," Marie Esteben said.

Capp stood inside the doorway of the apartment and looked at her. Raul had described her as perceptive, and she was. Capp knew she had read or heard about Whitencroft's death, and she suspected what her husband was doing the day he died. She'd known more about her husband than Raul had supposed. What else might she perceive behind that dark, measured gaze?

"I often do the unexpected," Capp said.

"Oh, but you don't. Why have you come here?"

There was idle curiosity in her voice, and something bordering disturbingly on pity. Capp crossed the apartment and turned in the center of the room to face her. "I needed to talk to you, to find out if anything's happened I should know about since I last saw you."

"You might have phoned. But then phones are toys you distrust."

"With reason."

"But you took the greater risk coming here in person. You violated one of your rules."

Capp knew she was right. "Why do you say that?"

"You know why." Marie refused to let him be evasive. "And you know the danger."

"What do you mean?"

"Nothing that matters." She had on a cheap blue dress with a broken belt loop and gaps between the pearl buttons that ran to her collar. She crossed her bare arms and stood gracefully with a hip out and her weight on one leg.

"Everyone needs to care about something, Marie."

"Do you, Wilson? Or do you need something to care about?"

"It's a fine distinction."

"But a distinction." She lowered her arms and took a few steps nearer to Capp. "Raul was like you. They made him that way, with their half-baked, self-serving philosophies he was always quoting. He was like a donkey chasing a carrot on a string. And when the carrot was gone, he continued to see it. He needed to continue the chase. The whole charade gave him a purpose."

"You're wrong, Marie."

"There is no such thing."

From either downstairs or outside came the distant voice of a man shouting something angrily in Spanish. He repeated whatever he'd shouted two more times, almost as if it were a pacifying litany. The yellowed curtains hung without movement in the thick, still morning air, giving Capp the impression that if he touched them he would find them to be of some rigid substance rather than cloth. A horn honked below in the street; more distant incoherent shouting. The tiny apartment seemed to be a module of quiet in the midst of an active world. Marie had to be lonely here.

Capp sat down on the sofa as if suddenly and unaccountably weary. He wondered himself why he'd really come here. Perhaps subconsciously he knew that he and Raul had involved themselves only in a complex but meaningless series of personal challenges. The means rather than the professed end might have been the mainspring of their lives. As it was with Berwin.

"Soon after you left here the last time," Marie said, "a man named Clyde Hawker came. He said he was with the FBI."

"Do you think he was what he claimed?"

"I'm not sure. He showed identification." She shrugged. "He asked me about Raul."

"What did he look like?"

"He was a short man, with blue eyes, a very high, almost freakishly rounded forehead and a long, sharp chin. In his forties, I would say, tending to get fat about the middle. Very large tobacco-stained hands."

Capp had to smile at the thoroughness of the description. It was unlikely that this man, with such pronounced physical characteristics, was the man who'd been asking about Julian in Cincinnati. Capp's actions had created ripples reaching far beyond his expectations, his control. He hadn't known about Lazarus.

Things ponderous and unknown were moving about him, and perhaps that was why he'd come here, to Marie Esteben's apartment, where there existed the illusion that time and the inexorable had ceased their concentric, increasing power over him. He was aware that the flesh at the right corner of his mouth was ticking rapidly.

Marie was standing watching him. A familiar, acrid scent wafted in from the kitchen. Something, perhaps her breakfast toast, was burning. Marie ignored the smell and came to the sofa to sit next to him.

"On the coast of San Sangrar, where I come from in Cuba," she told him, "there is a place where the ocean breaks on flat beach. When the fishermen attempt to put to sea in their small boats the strong undertow and the crash of the sea drive them back to shore unless they struggle very hard. But when they reach a certain point, beyond the undertow, it is difficult to do anything but continue out to sea. You have passed that point, Wilson."

"I know," he told her. His voice broke, but with a tremor he gained control of himself. "That's why I came here. And that's why I have to leave."

Marie placed a cool, steady hand on his cheek and applied gentle pressure so that his head rested on her shoulder. "You are just like Raul." She stroked his hair lightly with the very tips of her fingers. "You can never give up." Incomprehension gleamed like a lost, bright coin in the depths of her eyes. "Never . . ."

Outside, the distant incoherent shouting began again.

⊠ 33

THERE'S ONLY ONE WAY now, Chereno thought, but he knew better than to say it aloud. Capp would have to die soon, and that implicit knowledge permeated the atmosphere in Andrew Berwin's office.

Chereno and Dwayne Stauker were seated in chairs near the wide walnut desk. Berwin was pacing, unconsciously lengthening his strides and bending his upper body forward.

"How could he have found out to begin with?" Berwin asked, as if some cunning card trick had been played on him and he was irritated.

Stauker crossed his ankle over his knee, adjusted a black silk sock and looked up at Berwin. "Capp was bound to tumble to it one way or another. He has that tilt of mind."

"We can deal with it," Chereno said.

"Yes, yes." Berwin nodded several times in rapid succession. "It needs to be dealt with decisively and immediately." He had on his sharp but fleshy features the look of a man who could see on the horizon dominoes falling in his direction. "I want progress reports twice daily from you," he said to Chereno. Then, to Stauker: "I need to be kept apprised of the overall strategy as it pertains to Lazarus. We have a time factor now."

Stauker patted a wayward strand of his tightly curled gray hair into place and nodded. Keeping his own expression placid, he watched the fear play over Berwin's face. Stauker knew that he might well be the domino preceding Berwin.

Berwin stopped pacing, sat down at his desk and began to

drum his fingers. The drumming became increasingly louder until suddenly he became aware of it and stopped, folding his hands so that they lay like high-strung pale animals at rest on the gleaming desk top. "Do you have all the help you need?" he asked Chereno.

"More would be a case of too many chefs in the kitchen," Chereno said. "Capp has to be dealt witn in a cautious, discreet manner. The men I have I can trust."

"And if you couldn't trust them, could you control them?"

"Yes."

"The murders have been progressive," Stauker said, "up the line of authority and responsibility, at least as Capp perceives that line. The question is, Will he return to Wellman?"

"I think he will," Chereno said. "Wellman is a loose end that Capp will never be able to tolerate. And Capp is a man nurturing a great need for vengeance to keep himself going. He won't leave Wellman for last. That would be like consuming an hors d'oeuvre after the main course."

"You sound more like a cook than what you are," Berwin said in agitation. He began to drum his fingertips again.

"I agree with him, though," Stauker said. "Capp sees himself as an instrument of justice and order. He won't leave Wellman for last. Wellman is the best bet to be the next victim."

"If we can't find Capp," Chereno said, "we can wait for him to come to Wellman."

Berwin's lips pursed. He almost said the word *bait* but did not. "You fellows know best how to do your jobs," he said. Then, as if speaking for the benefit of some unseen presence: "We don't want David Wellman hurt."

"He won't be," Stauker said.

But Chereno knew better. With Capp, there would always be risk. Chereno had a great deal of respect for Capp, even admiration, and he knew Capp would be almost impossible to find now that he was aware he was being pursued from more than one direction. It was the elusiveness of his quarry that made the Wellman idea seem like a good one to Chereno. And there was the time factor Berwin had mentioned: Capp might talk at any time into the wrong ear. The New York state primary was near, then the convention, the presidential campaign and election.

Berwin got up and walked to stand by the tall window. He was wearing a dark-blue pin-striped suit with padded squared shoulders. Fear seemed to instill in him an added awkward stiffness that contrasted with the sight of the breeze gracefully ruffling the curved distant palm fronds.

" 'Discreet' was the most important word you uttered." Apparently he was speaking to Chereno. "We mustn't let the bastards find out about this. For everyone's sake." He wheeled to face both seated listeners, his fists on his hips, jaw outthrust and aggressive. "They've erected every obstacle, fairly and unfairly, and we've overcome each and every one of them. We won't be stopped by this."

Chereno wondered if "this" referred to Capp or to Gateway, but he didn't ask.

Berwin said, "At any time either of you can come here to speak to me personally so that any point may be clarified. Phone first on the regular line and I'll clear you with the Secret Service. We're in an extremely delicate area of the operation, and I think when we get past this we'll have clear going. But we can't afford any misunderstandings." He licked his lips, then he gave up his aggressive stance, like an actor shedding a role, and stared flatly at both men.

"I'll be awaiting word," he said. He smiled a quick smile, then nodded briskly in dismissal.

Berwin was already seated at his desk reading a letter as Chereno and Stauker were going out the door.

When they were outside, near where their cars were parked angled toward the sea, Stauker laid a hand on Chereno's shoulder and Chereno turned to face him. Above the two men, low, wraithlike gray clouds scudded past. The surf pounded with a sluggish, irregular pulse.

"There's no need to mince words out here," Stauker said.

He manipulated cupped hands and lighter flame against the breeze. "When you find Capp, waste him at whatever cost. We can't afford to have him fall into anyone else's capable hands." Exhaled gray smoke whipped away in shreds behind Stauker.

"How much should I tell Wellman?"

"Don't tell him anything, but give him his protection. Capp would be suspicious if we didn't move to protect. But your job is Capp."

"I understand the priorities," Chereno said.

Stauker got into his chocolate-brown Mercedes and had the engine started before Chereno's hand was on the Dodge's pitted chrome door handle.

Chereno closed the door, seeming to pull in with it a calm silence that filled the car. He followed the gleaming Mercedes down the road toward the wide chain link gate. The guard glanced at them, worked the controls that opened the imposing gate, then waved them through.

As the Mercedes pulled away from Chereno on the narrow blacktop road, he wondered if anywhere in this world there lived someone who wasn't expendable.

Not likely, he decided. It was a foregone conclusion that no one lived forever.

☒ 34

CHERENO DROVE AROUND the block again, slowing as he passed the Belmont Towers. He had examined the New York apartment building itself, including David Wellman's unit, earlier that afternoon. Now it was the neighborhood that interested him. He steered the Dodge to the curb lane and slowed even further.

Directly across from the Belmont Towers was a small all-night drugstore that appeared to sell mainly prescription medicine and paperback books. Down the street was Burger Bin, a short-order restaurant with a circular counter and a few tables. Then came the Regal Shoeshine Parlor, a cubbyhole establishment that was closed and appeared to have been boarded up for some time. The rest of the block was mostly office or apartment buildings, and at the corner was a small tavern called Chances Aren't. Chereno jotted down the address of the closed shoeshine parlor and pulled back into the sporadic stream of traffic on Fourth Street.

He parked the Dodge around the corner on St. Charles, then walked back to the Belmont Towers. In the lobby he made two brief calls on the public phone before crossing the scuffed marbled floor to the elevators. One of the elevators was at lobby level, its doors gaping. Chereno stepped inside and pressed the *17* button.

Martin and Carlos, the same men who had guarded Whitencroft, were in 17-E with Wellman. They were standing relaxed in the living room. Wellman was sitting on the sofa where he'd sat when Capp and Julian had interrogated him. After Martin had admitted Chereno, he continued to stand near the door.

"You follow instructions, Mr. Wellman," Chereno said, "and you'll stay safe till Capp is found."

Wellman was apprehensive. His going-to-gray hair was unevenly parted and most of the color had left his full cheeks. He was wearing dark slacks and a blue-and-green print silky sport shirt cut square at the hem and hanging outside his belt. As he sat, his right hand was twisting the tail of the shirt and pulling it tight across his tense body. "Jesus! . . ." he said. "When I heard about Alex . . ."

"Whitencroft didn't follow instructions," Chereno said, "or he'd still be alive. He'd been told to stay off the balcony."

Carlos was silently nodding his narrow, alert head in sullen agreement. Martin remained standing near the door.

"You figure Capp will really come back here?" Wellman asked. His tone of voice suggested that he was seeking reassurance in a negative answer.

Chereno said, "I doubt it. But you wanted protection and it's being provided. It does no harm to take precautions, and we can take them for you. Just go about your business as if nothing were wrong. Martin or Carlos will be around."

"Can you get back to Berwin that I appreciate this?"

"Certainly."

Wellman stopped twisting the silky material of his shirt and stood up. He slid his hands into his back pockets and stared up at the ceiling. "I wish to Christ this were over." After a long sigh, he lowered his head to look at Chereno. "You know anything about Wilson Capp?"

"What I need to know," Chereno said.

"Is he as good as his record indicates?"

"Probably better. But then I am as effective."

The words had been spoken seriously and Wellman seemed to derive confidence from them. He unconsciously smoothed the wrinkled material of his shirt.

"You don't have to stay cooped up here," Chereno told him. "Your protection moves with you."

"But won't it be safer here?"

"Not necessarily. If Capp follows you he'll be spotted. And here he knows where to find you. If Whitencroft had been out surrounded by people, he might still be alive."

Wellman's moon face clouded again with worry; lately he seemed to be assailed by a preponderance of ifs.

"This shouldn't have to last long," Chereno said smoothly. "A week, maybe two at the most."

Wellman nodded automatically, without conviction.

"Martin will stay here with you," Chereno said. "Carlos will be down in the lobby. You'll hardly know they're around, but they will be."

Chereno gave Wellman a confident pat on the arm, then motioned with his head to Carlos. Wellman showed them out.

Chereno and Carlos rode down together in the old elevator, and Chereno left the Cuban standing and smoking in the lobby. As he walked from the Belmont Towers, it inanely occurred to Chereno that Carlos, who was a chain smoker, would add immeasurably to the array of dark burn marks from extinguished cigarette butts on the marble floor.

Outside, Chereno walked past the dim, cavernous exit from the Belmont Towers' underground garage, where Wellman's car was parked in its private slot, and around the corner to where his Dodge was parked at the curb. He wondered if Capp would actually try again so soon for Wellman. Capp would be aware that every precaution had been taken to protect his target, but the situation being what it was, that fact might only whet his appetite. All armor had chinks, and Capp was the canny professional who could find and exploit them.

But it was to Chereno's advantage that he understood something about Capp that Berwin and perhaps even Stauker did not: Capp would not see Wellman so much as a debt unsettled as a job unfinished. It was the latter that Capp would never be able to walk away from.

And Chereno understood something that Capp didn't. He understood how to live with the thing that inevitably grew in those who killed too often in too short a period, that took root in the groin and wended its way to the heart and the darkest corners of the mind.

Chereno got into his car and drove away, wondering how soon he'd be able to return.

He was back within an hour, with a bag containing four McDonald's hamburgers in their insulating styrofoam containers, a large thermos of hot coffee and a key. He fitted the key to the door of the deserted Regal Shoeshine Parlor and let himself in, pressing with the weight of his body to spring the few long nails driven at random through paint-checked wood.

The inside of the shoeshine parlor was dim and musty. In the shadows Chereno could make out a few wooden chairs arranged atop a low platform with jutting metal supports where long-ago customers had rested the soles of their shoes. Some cardboard boxes were piled along the back wall in jumbled disarray. From outside, Chereno had thought the small show window was soaped, but now he realized that the window was simply coated with a layer of dirt. He used his palm to rub a clear spot beneath the g in *Regal,* got one of the wood folding chairs from the platform along the wall and settled down to watch the entrance of the Belmont Towers across the street.

The interior of Chances Aren't, on the corner of Fourth and Mission, was illuminated only by flickering artificial candles set in fixtures along baroque walls, and by the steady glow of the neon Schlitz beer sign behind the long upholstered bar. The sign depicted an attractive brunette water-skiing, body arched back, legs slightly angled, twisted at the waist to smile and wave toward the bar with one hand while holding tight to the tow rope handle with the other. The illuminated blue from the parted water cast a pale light over the three solitary drinkers at the bar.

An ancient ornate jukebox sat dead and unlighted in a corner; the only sounds were those of a softly playing radio tuned to a ball game, and the muted murmurings of a couple in a booth near the door. The only drinker at the tables in Chances Aren't was a man sitting nursing a beer while he strained to read a magazine.

Chances Aren't didn't supply table service. Clyde Hawker went to the bar and ordered a draft beer from the wizened, unsmiling bartender. The beer flowed into the stein from a chrome tap, interrupted only by hesitation on the handle when a base hit drove in a run. Hawker paid for his beer and carried the overflowing stein to a table near the window. He positioned his chair carefully, sat down and visibly relaxed, a man settling in for a wait.

From his vantage point on the corner Hawker could barely see the entrance of the Belmont Towers, but he had a clear view of one of the underground garage's exits and a partial view of the other at the side of the building.

Hawker knew he could sit here until closing time, then continue his surveillance from his parked car. It was an act of providence that the jukebox was broken or unplugged. He hated to subject himself to the mindless, raucous rhythms that passed for rock music, or to the sugary, simple sentimentalism of country songs. He missed Frankie Laine.

He sighed with what satisfaction he could muster in his job. He had a good line on the Belmont Towers and could even see the lighted window of Wellman's seventeenth-floor apartment. And the beer was cold enough to contain flecks of ice, the way he liked it.

☒ 35

The senator sipped his manhattan on the rocks, then inserted the glass into its special gyroscopic holder alongside the seat in his private compartment. If the converted Boeing 707 dipped or was buffeted by rough air, while the plane tilted the glass would remain level on its system of concentric rings riding on precision bearings.

The 707 had been loaned by Vulcast Industries to aid in the senator's campaign for the presidency. Vulcast was a conglomerate of which the senator was a major stockholder. From the outset he had made no excuses for his wealth; after all, he had begun poor. And if elected all his assets would be placed in a blind trust. He didn't feel that his wealth had so far hurt him in his search for votes. If a Rockefeller could aspire to the presidency, so could he. Next to a Rockefeller, the senator was a pauper. And, as he liked to point out, his total assets actually were only 20 percent more than those of his principal opponent in the battle for the nomination.

The senator's private compartment was located on the right side of the plane's fuselage, in front of the wing. It was carpeted in plush beige, equipped with a wet bar, a sofa that converted to a double bunk, a leather-upholstered seat wherein he now sat, and a small desk with a swing-away stool.

Abruptly the plane dropped a few feet in a pressure pocket, causing the blue capsules on the tray before the senator to roll in wobbly, erratic patterns yet somehow avoid each other. The capsules contained secobarbital, which the senator took at times to help him sleep. Enough of the capsules washed down with what would be his fourth manhattan would prove fatal. The senator was considering swallowing the capsules.

For hours his mind had been exploring, darting desperately, like a trapped insect probing a clear but unyielding pane of glass, trying to find a way through, over, under, around. But there was no way to the other side of the glass. Berwin had him.

It had seemed unlikely that Berwin's promises could be fulfilled, the favoritism, the money delivered, the series of misfortunes to opponents. The senator had really never dreamed it would carry him this far, to here, to the brink of the presidency.

Of course, he'd never for a moment doubted the sincerity or potency of the implied threats. Berwin was in an unassailable position to exert pressure, to gain control of the senator's campaign, and no one would be as ruthless as Berwin with his secret information.

At first cooperation had seemed not simply the only course but a course the senator could eventually adjust to, could live with. Every politician, every president, is to some degree inconveniently beholden. But he'd never dreamed the last seven months would exact such a price from him.

Whichever way he moved, whichever direction he turned, he was blocked by an irresistible, uncompromising obstruction. Always there was only one clear avenue, and that was the avenue Berwin had chosen. And his concern with Berwin had lately blossomed into something that in the beginning he should have suspected but wouldn't allow himself to consider.

The senator was becoming increasingly suspicious that Berwin was no longer rational.

A faint vibration ran steadily through the 707, and the muted roar of the engines was constant and hypnotic. The senator sat and watched the oval capsules trace their now regular, predictable patterns on the flat terrain of the tray. He picked up one of the tiny capsules and raised it to his lips.

Then he placed the capsule back on the tray.

He sat with his fingertips resting against his forehead, his eyes closed, his lips moving silently.

After a while the senator opened his eyes and one by one replaced the capsules in their bottle and resealed the cap. He picked up his drink and sat holding it with both hands, staring out the compartment window. If he hadn't the courage to swallow the capsules, did he have the courage to function as President of a powerful, troubled nation? Courage was courage, in either case. Only a hypocrite could think otherwise.

The senator sat staring down through the clear night at the lights of the cities gliding beneath him, feeling detached and lost. And frightened.

So very frightened.

☒ 36

Capp had taken a room at the Hotel Majestic in New York, a dilapidated brick building that, like so many of its tenants, had outlived its prime years. Its seedy, impersonal rooms, its echoing halls with their antiquated ceiling fixtures, its worn lobby with its ancient oak desk and soiled leather registration book, all gave off an aura of the sort of loneliness that maims.

The Majestic was on Dennen Street between Cass and Locust, on the edge of an area of Manhattan due to be razed soon to make way for a new convention center. From his tenth-floor room Capp had a view of blocks of vacant, half-demolished buildings with rows of glassless blank windows. After the first day he kept the yellowed venetian blinds slanted to admit only thin cracks of light from above.

Capp had taken one of the more expensive rooms, equipped with an old black-and-white TV set that still worked. But there was nothing on TV during the day that he cared to watch, and the room made him uneasy. Indecipherable sounds sang through the old pipes and there seemed to be a light haze in the air when he looked toward the window, as if something unseen in the room were continually stirring and keeping the dust aloft. On the pale-green wall near the head of the bed were the darkened remains of a smashed insect.

At times Capp regretted not taking a room at one of the better hotels, but he wanted to vary his habits. And the Hotel Majestic was strategically located.

He knew that very shortly the room would seem like a refuge, but right now he needed to get out.

On the nearby corner of Cass and Grant was a small coffee shop with a newspaper vending machine outside its door. Maybe he would still be able to get a morning paper. He shrugged into his wrinkled sport coat and left, locking the door carefully behind him and inserting a paper match between door and frame near the floor so he'd know if anyone had entered in his absence. Not that the match would do much good; whoever might locate the room would be sure to check the door before entering. But the precaution cost Capp nothing.

There was a newspaper vending machine that he hadn't noticed in the lobby. The desk man, a redheaded troll, glanced at him without seeing him as Capp inserted his coin and withdrew the last paper. The Majestic was the sort of hotel where memories are deliberately short and inaccurate. Capp tucked the paper beneath his left arm and walked toward Grant Street.

The neighborhood was mixed but predominantly black. There were few cars on the streets; the desolation from the nearby area slated for demolition seemed to have spread like an infection. On Cass Avenue a man in a long tan topcoat approached Capp. It was only when the man drew near that Capp saw that the coat was soiled and threadbare, and that the man had on mud-caked shoes. The man studied Capp for a moment, bleary-eyed and unshaven, as if considering asking for a handout. Then he seemed to decide that Capp wasn't all that much better off than himself and walked past, muttering something Capp couldn't understand.

The coffee shop was a place of white enamel, spotted glass and bright stainless steel. Inside, it was surprisingly clean. Capp decided that it derived most of its business from a nearby bus stop. Perhaps the bus stop was even responsible for the name Stop 'n' Snack. Vaguer things had happened.

A tall thin man stood behind the counter scraping the grill. The tangy scent of fried bacon was in the air. Capp was the only customer. Behind the counter a handwritten menu listed half a dozen breakfasts and two sizes for coffee and juice. The tall man raised inquisitive sandy eyebrows. He had a sad face and a graying mustache that partly hid the deep scar running crosswise on his sallow cheek.

"Coffee black and a glazed doughnut," Capp said, sliding onto a stool.

The man poured the coffee first, then carefully set the doughnut like a display model on a napkin in front of Capp. He turned back to scraping what looked like caked bacon grease from the grill.

The coffee was hot and good, the doughnut fresh. After a few sips and bites, Capp spread his newspaper on the counter and hunched over it.

The press was now all but naming him as the killer of the four former White House staff or cabinet members. And he read that Andrew Berwin had demanded and received additional Secret Service protection.

In a way Capp was glad it had all come out in the open. Now Myra and Bess would be safe from Berwin and Stauker. Any harm that might come to Capp's family would be all too obvious a move, bringing about a thorough and vigorous investigation that might uncover Lazarus. Right now Capp didn't want that to happen any more than Berwin did. He didn't want Berwin attracting publicity, being surrounded by the press or even taken into custody where Capp couldn't reach him.

Capp took a sip of coffee. The rest of the front page was filled with news of the presidential campaigns. There was much speculation, much editorializing. Ordinarily it was tough to defeat an incumbent, but not this time. Too many mistakes had been made, and the President had committed what to the voters is the one unforgivable sin: he had projected an image of incompetence. In the final analysis, that had also been Berwin's mistake.

"It's some joke, ain't it?" the scarred man behind the counter said. He had left the spatula propped on the cooling grill and was wiping down the counter top. "I mean, all these guys runnin' for president like we had some real choice in the matter." He'd glanced at Capp's newspaper, at the front-page photo of Senator Walter Temple smiling and waving with the Statue of Liberty in the background over his left shoulder.

Capp took a bite of the glazed doughnut.

"I mean, it ain't like one's not a bigger crook than the other," the scarred man continued, rhythmically working the white towel on the smooth counter top. "Everybody knows they're all alike; they got to be that way to get where they are, now don't they?"

"Maybe you're right," Capp said. He didn't want to be remembered for his silence.

The neatly folded towel paused, then continued in its regular, circular motion. "You take Berwin. He wasn't no worse than most, no worse than what we got now. Only thing is, he got caught, you know? We don't know what goes on now, 'cause we got us a new set of crooks. Now, in November we can keep them or we can vote to change the game. But the game will still be rigged, you know?"

"I know." Capp did know.

The scarred man backed away from the counter. He picked up a round glass coffeepot from the burner and poured Capp a warm-up. Outside a bus went by with a resonant bass hum that vibrated the plate glass window. Capp wished another customer would come into the Stop 'n' Snack, but no one did. The topcoated man Capp had seen on Cass Avenue shambled past on the other side of the street, staring straight ahead.

Capp worked on his cup of coffee and pretended to be absorbed in the newspaper, wondering what security measures had been added at Lost Palms. But he was getting ahead of himself; there was a time for looking into the future, but now wasn't it. The present was problem enough.

"You think I'm gonna vote?" the scarred man behind the

counter asked, pouring himself a cup of coffee.

Capp continued to stare down at the newspaper. "I don't know."

"I'm not. It don't matter. I found that out through the years. It don't matter."

The words rang with disturbing familiarity. They had been spoken in the same tone Marie Esteben had used, not defiant, not resigned; the words had been said with the same solidified conviction that someone might convey when stating that the world was round or that gravity made things fall.

"It's a knot nobody can untangle, you know?" the counterman said.

Now the coffee shop door did open and a short black woman in an absurd shaggy gray fur coat entered. The obviously artificial head of some unspecified small animal dangled from the back of the wide collar as she sat on a stool at the end of the counter.

Capp laid a bill on the counter and walked out as the scarred man was taking the black woman's order. Another bus went past, almost empty, trailing lingering diesel fumes. He'd deliberately left the paper behind on the counter top, folded to the sports page.

Capp walked east on Grant Street, glancing at his watch. In two hours he was to meet Julian. He slipped his hand into his pants pocket and fingered the room key with its engraved plastic tag. Feeling the tag brought to mind the drab green oppressiveness of room 1034 at the Hotel Majestic. Capp didn't want to return there yet.

He walked for several blocks, to the fringes of the business district and shopping area. There were more people on the sidewalk now, and Capp was inconspicuous. There still were a great many blacks, and some Spanish or Puerto Ricans, among the pedestrians. The faces of the people who passed seemed preoccupied but untroubled. It had always seemed incongruous to Capp that his craft was practiced among unsuspecting people going about the daily business of their lives, but never so incongruous as now.

Capp walked idly about for some time, gazing into display windows, glimpsing passing faces, catching snatches of seemingly inane conversation.

Then he found himself only a few blocks from the Hotel Majestic, and he finally admitted to himself that he had nowhere else to go.

☒ 37

THERE WERE MANY PLACES Chereno would rather have been than inside the deserted Regal Shoeshine Parlor. The place had a dampness to it that made him constantly uncomfortable, and he now and then caught a scent of what could only be the pungent stale waxiness of leather polish. Once a scurrying in the jumble of cardboard boxes in the dimness behind him startled him, but he decided the sound must have been made by a mouse or rat.

The shadows on Fourth Street were lengthening as dusk settled among the buildings. An elderly gray-haired woman whom Chereno had seen before entered the Belmont Towers. She was a widow who lived on the second floor and always went out in the afternoons and returned at about this time. A few cars whizzed past, temporarily blocking Chereno's view into the lobby, where Carlos was stationed. Preceded by strident chattering, two teen-aged girls strutted past the Regal Shoeshine Parlor, briefly checking their reflections in the dirt-smeared window. They walked on, giggling and trailing long distorted shadows that themselves seemed youthful. A red Ford Pinto emerged from the basement garage of the Belmont Towers, made a left onto Fourth and accelerated, its young male driver glancing with ludicrous appraisal at the two girls.

This was the third day of the watch on Wellman. Chereno was becoming mildly impatient. What might Capp be doing if they'd guessed wrong and were wasting their time here?

The small leather-encased walkie-talkie on the floor next to Chereno's chair emitted a low crackling sound, like crumpling cellophane.

Martin's voice was concise and loud in the quiet dimness. "Going out by car."

Chereno picked up the walkie-talkie and pressed the transmit button. "Acknowledged."

Standing stiffly, Chereno slipped the walkie-talkie into the side pocket of his suit coat. He dusted off the seat of his pants, then left the Regal Shoeshine Parlor, locking the door behind him. Casually he walked to where his car was parked, got in and started the engine.

Within half a minute Wellman's black Chevy emerged, a sleek thing launched from the dark exit of the Belmont Towers garage, and made a cautious right turn to blend with the traffic. Carlos, driving a rented gray Ford, was close behind Wellman, then dropped back a discreet distance and allowed a car to edge in ahead of him. There were few better at trailing in heavy traffic than Carlos.

Chereno waited until both cars had passed, then pulled the Dodge away from the curb. He stayed as far back as possible while still being able to keep tabs on the two automobiles. It was easy for him because he knew where Wellman was going: to the Celtic Cafeteria, a large bustling restaurant on Reever Avenue where he could eat supper surrounded by people and comforted by the knowledge that Carlos was nearby. This was the third night in a row that Wellman had eaten at the same restaurant, which was in itself a bad idea. But Chereno didn't tell Wellman that.

The setting sun touched the thick air with faint, merging bands of color. Chereno reached down and flicked on his headlights. This was the time of day when the light played tricks, interfered with depth perception and contour. The exhaust fumes of the cars ahead of Chereno added to the wavering dusk. He made a left turn, barely avoiding the wink of a red traffic light. The growl in the Dodge's differential was gradually becoming louder. He'd have to get it repaired soon, he told himself, or start scouting for another car.

They were in a busy section of town now; quite a few

people roamed the wide sidewalks and traffic was heavier. The gray rear fender of Carlos's Ford was barely visible at a stop sign a block ahead. A cab cut in front of a car coming the other way, as if making a left turn on a whim, and drew three short, angry horn blasts.

It was on Tenth Street that Chereno saw the tan Plymouth. The car drew his attention immediately. He'd noticed it yesterday behind Wellman's car on the way back from the restaurant. Chereno was sure it was the same car, the same man driving. Automatically he memorized the Plymouth's license number.

The rest of the way to the cafeteria Chereno stayed behind the Plymouth. Several times, in the congestion of downtown traffic near Sixth Avenue, both Chereno and the Plymouth passed Carlos.

By the time they reached the restaurant, Chereno was sure the man in the Plymouth was following Wellman but wasn't aware of Carlos.

The man stayed inside the Plymouth, parked on the cafeteria's blacktop lot, while Wellman had supper. Chereno parked on the street half a block up from the phony stucco-and-wood-beam Tudor restaurant. A red neon coat of arms glowed in dim distorted miniature on the blue hood of his car.

Forty-five minutes later Wellman came out of the restaurant with Carlos half a step behind him. Carlos hitched up his belt and walked in the manner of a man well fed, but Chereno knew he'd already caught sight of the man in the parked Plymouth and was watching him closely.

Carlos stayed on Wellman's rear bumper as their cars pulled from the lot, then in the comparative safety of the street let Wellman pull farther ahead of him. The tan Plymouth vibrated as its motor started, then lurched into reverse to back out of its parking slot and lurched forward as it headed for the driveway.

Chereno hit the transmit button on his walkie-talkie and

told Carlos to return by another route. Then he tugged on the car's transmission lever and pulled away from the curb to follow the tan Plymouth.

Half an hour later, Chereno was standing with Carlos and Martin in the Belmont Towers lobby. Wellman was safely locked inside his apartment upstairs.

"He followed Wellman to and from the restaurant," Chereno said. "He's got the building staked out from the tavern down the street."

Martin's heavy-lidded eyes were wary. "What about the car?"

"According to the plate number, it's a rental."

Carlos lit a cigarette from the tip of the one he'd smoked down and looked without blinking through the haze at Chereno. "Capp's man?"

"It's possible, but I don't think so. He seems to be watching, like I am. I've never seen him before."

The three men stood silently for a moment in the quiet, marbled lobby. There were several possibilities as to whom the man in the tan Plymouth might represent, and all of them presented complications.

"I shouldn't need to tell you," Chereno said, "that we don't inform Wellman about this interested party."

Martin smiled lazily. "You didn't need to tell us." Slowly he reached around and began to massage the back of his broad neck. All of his movements seemed languid, potent with checked power.

"We'll continue as before," Chereno said. "But be advised our friend is with us."

Chereno waited until Martin had started back upstairs in the noisy, faltering elevator before walking from the lobby and crossing the street.

Wellman went out briefly the next morning to speak to

someone at his bank. The man in the tan Plymouth followed him there and back, then took up his station inside Chances Aren't.

The rest of the day Wellman stayed inside his apartment, and Chereno stayed inside the Regal Shoeshine Parlor and sipped enough coffee from his thermos to give him a persistent stomachache.

As evening was nearing, Chereno peered through his clear spot on the dirty window and saw the gray-haired woman from the second floor enter the Belmont Towers. And there was an unshaven down-and-outer in a long baggy coat leaning against the brick wall, occasionally accosting likely-looking passersby for handouts. Chereno had seen the man at that same spot before and paid him little attention.

A taxi pulled up in front of the building and let out a heavy-set woman and a little girl with long braids. Clipped to the sides of the girl's head were shiny metal barrettes that caught the dying light in shots of silver as she moved. The woman paid the driver and the taxi sped off as she and the girl climbed the entrance steps, the girl flouncing and tossing her braids.

Chereno sensed something was wrong the instant the woman and girl had disappeared inside.

The man in the long coat was gone.

Chereno left his chair and craned forward toward the dirt-smeared window. The man was nowhere in sight, in either direction. It had taken less than twenty seconds for the woman and little girl to emerge from the cab and go inside—not enough time for the man to move out of sight.

Unless . . .

Unless he'd gone into the shadowed exit of the Belmont Towers' underground garage!

Chereno knocked over his chair as he crossed the room and let himself out of the shoeshine parlor. He ran across the street, then slowed as he walked down the steep cement drive to the parking area.

The underground garage was large, the building above it

supported by thick cement pillars striped in faded yellow. Overhead fixtures, many of which were burned out, provided little light. There were about twenty cars angled into their private parking slots about the garage.

From the shadows inside the entranceway, Chereno glanced over at the elevators, saw nothing. Slowly he worked his way along the cool cement wall toward where Wellman's car was parked. It could be that the bum had merely ducked into the garage to take a nip from a bottle, or to relieve himself. Or it could be that he wasn't a bum at all and was waiting for Wellman to come down for his car to drive out for supper as he'd done the past three evenings about this time.

The cavernous garage was cool, the smooth floor stained by countless oil drippings. There was a strong smell of grease and from somewhere came the sound of water slowly dripping onto cement. Chereno moved out from the wall to ease around a dusty red fire extinguisher mounted on metal brackets.

When he was about fifty feet from Wellman's Chevrolet, he saw the disheveled figure of the panhandler straighten to raise its head above the curved roofline of the car and glance around the garage. Chereno stood still, mentally merging himself with the shadows.

He let out his breath slowly, sure that the man hadn't seen him.

What was the man doing now, writhing about to cast faint multiple shadows? He was removing his bulky coat.

Chereno watched him carefully wad up the coat, reach through the window and lay it in the car, then walk hurriedly away. The stark coatless silhouette of the man appeared for a moment framed in the side exit of the garage as he hurried up the ramp and turned to walk toward Fourth Street.

Chereno waited a moment, then followed, not worrying now about the echoing loudness of his footsteps.

Outside the building, he tried briefly to alert Carlos and Martin with the walkie-talkie, but either he was out of range or something was jamming the transmission.

The man seemed to be in no hurry now and didn't once glance behind him.

Exactly fifteen minutes after Chereno had followed the man from the Belmont Towers' basement garage, Wellman's car exploded.

The blast rocked the old building, causing one of the cracked stone sea nymphs at the entrance to topple and lose an arm and half its face. The dim underground garage was illuminated for a second as if by a lightning flash, and a billow of dark smoke rolled from one of the garage entrances, hung low, then began to rise straight up and dissipate into a receptive graying sky. A woman shrieked her terror as if to release it to rise with the smoke.

In the Belmont Towers lobby, Carlos recovered from the shock of the explosion beneath him, flicked away his cigarette and crushed it with his first step as he bolted for the stairs to the basement garage. He took the two flights of metal steps with unbalanced yet graceful leaps, supporting himself with one hand on the banister while with the other he drew a large automatic from his belt holster.

When he threw open the heavy gray door to the garage he saw Wellman's car, or what remained of it, burning. The hood was twisted and dangling by one hinge at the side of the car, and the force of the explosion had sprung the trunk and peeled back part of the metal roof. Carlos crouched to avoid breathing in the foul black smoke that hung in the now quiet garage.

There were a few dark figures about, standing still or moving toward the car, drawn by the sound of the explosion. Carlos holstered his gun and held his handkerchief over his nose and mouth as he moved as close as possible to the burning car. Through the smoke and flames he could see something huddled and dark on the front seat, licked by a halo of fire. The heat forced him to back away.

At the sound of the explosion and the rush of dark smoke

from the garage entrance, Clyde Hawker had left Chances Aren't and broken into a run. Even before he entered the garage and saw the burning car, he'd been fairly sure of the source of the explosion: this was the time when Wellman usually drove to the Celtic Cafeteria for supper.

The fire was brief though fierce. The flames had almost died completely when Hawker approached the blackened wreckage of the car. There were several people, most of them the building's tenants, gathered in a circle about the car and peering through the acrid lingering smoke. Had it not been for a blackened license plate, Hawker couldn't have been sure he was looking at what had been Wellman's car.

Some of the onlookers were moving closer now, with stunned but curious expressions. A woman in a pink dress and with pink foam rubber curlers in her hair stepped forward to peer in through the twisted window on the passenger's side.

A man near the rear of the car said, "Merciful Jesus, was anybody in there?" His eyes were glazed and bewildered.

The woman bent closer to the window, wrinkling her nose, her lips bloodless, bracing herself for what she might see.

And it occurred to Hawker that through the scent of burned rubber and heated metal he did not smell the cloying sweetness of charred flesh.

"Empty," the woman said. "Thank God it's empty. Must have been the gas tank."

Hawker saw an obviously shaken Latin man turn and head for the elevators, as if sickened by what he'd witnessed.

"Couldn't have been the gas tank," a voice pronounced authoritatively. "Gas tanks don't just explode."

"Whose car was it?"

"Whoever they are, they're lucky."

When Carlos let himself into Wellman's apartment he saw Martin lying unconscious near the couch. Martin's revolver was still in its shoulder holster, visible against the lustrous silk lining of his blue suit coat, and there was a vicious red welt raised on the side of his thick neck and extending into the dark hairline at the base of his skull. Carlos cursed in Spanish and moved past Martin's sprawled form into the bedroom.

Wellman was crouched in a corner by the neatly made bed with his knees drawn up. He seemed to be staring wildly at Carlos and had his hand raised in a palms-out halt signal. When Carlos looked closer he saw that Wellman's right thumb was caught between his throat and the knotted cord that had abruptly choked off his life.

Carlos turned his back on the body, calmly lit a cigarette, then tried to contact Chereno with his walkie-talkie. He received no answer.

He walked to the window and looked down and across Fourth Street at the abandoned face of the Regal Shoeshine Parlor, paying little attention to the slight, fashionably dressed man just rounding the corner.

Julian Zayas, who had done his work with his customary expedience, had disappeared.

☒ 38

IN HIS ROOM AT the Hotel Majestic, Capp sat on a stained sleeper sofa with his feet propped on a coffee table. The vinyl beneath his bare forearm was sticky with perspiration. At the opposite end of the sofa were two soiled throw pillows placed to cover an area where the sofa's yellowish batting was bulging out. The small, shaded lamp on an end table threw so little illumination that changes in camera shots on the old black-and-white TV intermittently altered the lighting in the room and played with the shadows.

After planting the explosives and coat in Wellman's car, Capp had returned here. He'd neither seen nor talked to Julian Zayas since that afternoon and had just learned on the evening news that Julian had succeeded and Wellman was dead.

But Capp hadn't experienced the usual satisfaction and sense of accomplishment.

The news anchorman led into a film account of a conference on the latest Middle East arms buildup, and the drab room brightened with a shot of rolling tanks against a wide desert and cloudless afternoon sky. Capp leaned forward, dark eyes squinting, as he heard the newscaster's words without grasping their import. A part of him knew he was really immersing himself in the news to escape his own worsening reality, to escape his loneliness and the tiny, tormenting burr of fear within him. What had seemed free will had only led further into the darkening morass that was beyond understanding. Capp didn't know why the news of Wellman's death had made him feel somehow diminished, and he was afraid.

The news was interrupted by two handsome elderly people whose chief problem in life seemed to be chronic irregularity. Their world was improved immeasurably by a popular laxative.

Capp looked away from the TV and saw Chereno.

Chereno had let himself in quietly and was standing a few feet inside the door, his stocky body relaxed and balanced. His gray plastic raincoat was sequined with droplets from the steady drizzle that had fallen for the past hour. He might have been smiling, but his face was so mapped with shadow-deepened lines in the soft light that it was difficult for Capp to be sure.

"You play by demanding rules," Chereno said, remaining motionless.

Chereno's stillness lent him a subtle unreality that heightened Capp's fear. Capp had known Walter Chereno well, but this man, while undeniably Chereno, was heavier, somehow different, older. Perhaps simply older.

Capp recovered with effort from his surprise, willed the tenseness from his body. He must have been followed from the Belmont Towers.

"Rules to live by," he said.

Chereno unmistakably smiled.

"But then we both know it isn't always that way," Capp said. "Or you wouldn't be here."

Chereno ignored Capp's observation. "You're mad with the madness of another time. But let's suppose you succeed in what you're trying to do, that you make it to the top. Then what, Wilson? What for you?"

"I can get Myra. We can fade. You know that."

Chereno laughed incredulously while his eyes remained fixed on Capp. "Maybe you could bring it off. You've brought off a lot the past month or so."

"Berwin hired you."

"As you well know." Chereno walked farther into the room, into the light cast by the small table lamp. He stayed between

Capp and the door. "The Wellman thing was clever, the bomb for a diversion at the time Wellman usually drove his car."

Capp didn't acknowledge the compliment.

Chereno took another short step forward. "But what if Wellman had decided to leave a few minutes early for dinner?"

"If Wellman was in the car when it blew up, all right. If he died in his apartment, all right. The only way he'd have been safe at the time of the explosion was if he was on his way down to his car, between apartment and garage. An acceptable risk."

"Apparently." There was a burst of sound from the TV as film of the fighting in South Africa was aired. Chereno's gaze didn't waver.

Capp figured that his one chance lay in the unexpected, and in dealing with Chereno that chance was microscopic. If Chereno moved just a few feet nearer, Capp's diversionary patter might allow the fraction of a second needed to reach Chereno before the stocky but quick man could react and draw a weapon. Capp would make his move in the middle of a sentence, a word . . . He shifted his feet so that when the time came he could move more quickly.

"No need for that," Chereno said in anticipation. He reached inside the gray plastic raincoat and withdrew a Colt .45 automatic. The smile again, a curiously immobile rearrangement of the deeply lined, square features. "You see, I've decided not to kill you."

On the news, one of the presidential candidates was earnestly stating his position on the problems of the aged. Chereno did a slow, precise sidestep and turned off the TV. Silence rushed into the room. Capp sat back, and the muzzle of the automatic was lowered.

"Do you know why I've decided not to follow instructions?" Chereno asked.

Capp nodded, resting an arm on the back of the sofa. The tips of his fingers touched the seam of one of the maroon throw pillows. He understood the inner workings of a man like Chereno. "Because Berwin's still operating, but not by our rules. Not when he can avoid them. That's been the trouble from the beginning."

"That's true," Chereno said. "There's no way to avoid the rules once you're caught up in them. They're rules of necessity."

"Exactly," Capp agreed. "And you're in the position I was in seven years ago. Berwin betrayed me. He might just as easily betray you. When all's said and done, he's a dangerous amateur. There's only one safe course with someone like that . . . rules of necessity." Capp paused, toying with the maroon throw pillow. "One thing, though . . ."

"I know," Chereno said, "Stauker. I'm afraid you'll have to give him up for what you want most. That is where we find ourselves."

"Directly to the head of the monster . . . not an unreasonable proposition." As he talked, Capp worked his hand beneath the round pillow. Now he casually reached across his body with his left hand and held the pillow wadded as if to silence the report of a gun that he'd worked up from between the sofa cushions.

Chereno seemed only mildly surprised when he glanced down and noticed the position and apparent purpose of the wadded pillow. There was always the possibility that a man like Capp wasn't bluffing.

"Now we start even," Capp said. "Tell me about Lazarus."

The silence in the room seemed to solidify and impede Chereno's breathing. Then he shrugged. "I've heard of Lazarus. I know very little about it. I see that I might as well sit down."

☒ 39

AT NINE IN THE EVENING TWO DAYS LATER, in a steamy Florida tropical rain, Chereno's blue Dodge approached the south gate of Lost Palms. A line of towering palm trees near the fence bent in elegant supplication to the storm, and gusts of wind shot the rain in dancing patterns across the car's hood. The Dodge stopped smoothly near the small guard shack whose fogged yellow windows revealed only shadowed movement within.

Capp was behind the car's steering wheel.

He was clean-shaven, wearing the dark-rimmed glasses that Chereno often wore, Chereno's gray raincoat and a brimmed tan rain hat. Chereno had advised approaching Lost Palms from this direction because of the added security forces. He was sure the men at the south gate had never seen him up close.

The man in the guard shack didn't realize the car had approached. Capp tapped the horn and rolled the window partway down. There was a sudden gust of wind and he could hear the palm fronds rattle overhead.

The guard was armed, a large government-issue revolver holstered to his side. Capp slipped into reverse and held the car steady with the brake.

The guard tipped the short bill of his rain cap as he approached, stepping nimbly to avoid a deep puddle. "Great night," he said.

Capp laughed. "For the fish." He handed the guard Chereno's identification.

Ignoring the steady rain, the guard stood studying the identification. Capp saw that he was young but very sure of himself, the type that would act quickly out of instinct as well as training. And act correctly. The guard handed back the identification, then walked toward the rear of the car to check the license number with a list he carried on a small clipboard. As he passed the rear side window, he automatically glanced in to check the backseat area of the car.

Capp watched him in the rearview mirror. The guard stood still for a moment with the clipboard braced against his stomach, his head cocked to one side as if he might be puzzled. Then he lowered the clipboard and walked out of range of the mirror.

The guard returned to his metal shack but left the door open. Capp could see a stool, a stand-up desk, and a small closed-circuit TV with a slowly panning black-and-white picture.

Ahead of Capp the tall chain-link gate swung open. He shifted back to drive, waved to the guard and drove through.

With his acceleration, the patter of raindrops on the shoulder of the plastic coat reminded Capp that he still had the window down. He gripped the top of the steering wheel with his right hand and cranked up the window with his left. The rhythmic deep thunking of the windshield wiper mechanism sounded through the interior of the car like an apprehensive heartbeat.

Capp's own heartbeat was accelerated as he maneuvered the car along the narrow, rain-slick blacktop. The long-familiar copper taste of fear coated the sides of his tongue. He knew he was enjoying himself.

As he made a banked left turn, Capp noticed a dark hunched figure in the rain, watching the road from beneath a bent palm tree, rifle expertly cradled. Chereno hadn't exaggerated about the security.

Ahead of Capp was the low stucco building that he'd seen only on newscasts. The structure seemed to hug the ground atop a slight rise, its few lighted windows like wary eyes. Lightning illuminated the area for a few seconds and the eyes went momentarily blank.

Capp parked at the side of the low building, as Chereno had directed. With the motor off, the windshield wipers still, he sat for a moment beneath the rain that noisily assaulted the car's metal roof. A coolness settled over him. He was close now to where he wanted to be, but what slight margin for error he'd possessed had disappeared. This was the way he liked it.

Quickly Capp got out of the car. The rain hit him with unexpected but welcome force. Raising his right hand both to hold his hat on and to conceal most of his face, he strode hurriedly toward where a Secret Service agent in a slicker stood by a door beneath a striped metal awning. The agent held the door open and Capp lowered his head, grasped his hat tighter in the gusting breeze and stepped inside.

Sudden silence.

Again Capp followed Chereno's directions. Two left turns, then a right, down the unadorned carpeted hall. He could barely hear thunder rumbling outside. As he walked, he removed the glasses and rain hat. When he came to a heavy wood door, Capp knocked, two short, three long. Thunder rumbled again as the storm outside made for the sea.

Andrew Berwin opened his office door.

If he had been smiling in greeting, the smile had quickly disappeared. Berwin was wearing neatly pressed navy blue slacks, a white shirt open at the collar with long sleeves rolled carefully to beneath the elbows. Inside the somehow stiffly informal attire, his body became suddenly rigid and ungainly. His sharp, sagging features took on a pallor and strange immobility, as if the flesh were coated with clear, hardening varnish. He staggered a few awkward steps backward and seemed to be restraining himself from bolting in terror.

Capp walked into the office, noticing the tall window, red plush carpeting, the gas fire dancing in the stone fireplace. Some legal-size lined yellow papers were fanned out on Berwin's polished walnut desk, crisscrossed by a gold ballpoint pen. The shaded desk lamp, an ornately etched brass globe on a wood base, provided the only illumination other than the flickering glow of the fire.

Berwin had retreated to behind the wide desk. He slumped into his leather desk chair and with obvious effort managed his stiff smile.

"Mr. Capp," he said. He cleared his throat. "To what do we owe this surprising visit?"

Capp removed his coat, and despite its wetness draped it over the arm of a black leather chair. He placed the rain hat atop the chair back.

"I'm here because no matter who you are, you're accountable for what you've done," Capp said. "You can't place yourself above the law without placing yourself outside it. And outside, where you are now, the rules apply more rigidly than inside. Mr. Chereno and I concluded that you aren't to be trusted."

A nervous sincerity that faintly alarmed Capp fluctuated in Berwin's strained smile. "What I've done? I don't understand . . ."

"It isn't you who doesn't understand, Mr. President."

Capp started at the sound of the voice, then stood very still.

When he slowly turned he saw Chereno step forward from the shadowed alcove where he'd been concealed. His ancient Colt automatic was leveled at Capp. He was smiling his incredibly lined smile.

"Don't act so unbefittingly surprised," he said to Capp. "I've been here since yesterday." He motioned with his head toward Berwin. "Meet Lazarus. You have to trust someone. This way there'll be no doubt as to your guilt and intentions, no questions leading to more questions."

A clap of thunder sounded like a near artillery report; the center of the storm was moving nearer. Lightning illuminated the office through the tall window.

Capp felt his fear settle icily deep in his bowels, a resigned, fatalistic fear he had never known.

"It was the Lazarus operation that you interfered with," Berwin said to Capp. "That was the real worry you presented."

"I would like to know," Capp said in a calm voice that couldn't have been his, "who is the Lazarus candidate?"

Berwin licked the corner of his mouth and flashed a toothy smile as another spear of lightning charged the night sky with brilliance. Capp counted the seconds between the lightning and the accompanying clap of thunder.

Berwin's rigid features glowed with a smug intensity. "If knowledge is power, Mr. Capp, then secret knowledge is power tenfold. But since you're highly unlikely to leak the information, it's Senator Adam Haller."

"Haller's a member of the opposition party."

"Insignificant."

"And he's the front runner."

"Now that, Mr. Capp, is what is significant. And we intend to see that he remains the front runner, because in a very real sense, it means that I am the front runner. I will become what might be described as the power behind the throne. And then, who knows? . . . Oh, I have plans, a destiny my enemies cannot deny me. Dreams can indeed come true for the determined dreamer, Mr. Capp, the rare dreamer with the courage to act on his vision."

Berwin's eyes left Capp, dismissed him as if he'd suddenly become inanimate, and Capp knew that the hunched and nervous little somber man behind the desk already regarded him as dead.

"Remember," Berwin said to Chereno, "he somehow got through the protective ring. As far as anyone knows, you're the one who just arrived in your car and coat. That's imperative."

Another bright lightning flash, and Capp began his count.

Chereno parted his lips to speak.

Thunder exploded through the night with an underlying, whiplike crack that sent sharp vibrations through the building.

Timing his move so that the clap of thunder, unexpected by Chereno and Berwin, would momentarily freeze the two men and give him the vital split second he needed, Capp took a long, racing step and hurled himself at the tall window. In midair he crossed his arms over his face, felt a numbing jolt and a merciful giving way as the glass shattered.

Capp landed running in a spray of broken glass, the rain suddenly cool on his face. Even then he knew it hadn't worked. Chereno was too much the professional to be startled by such a move.

Within three strides Capp felt two sharp, painful bites in his back, and something that gently brushed the side of his face in passing made a soft cracking sound in his ear. He heard his own high, gasping intake of breath.

But Capp had made the darkness.

More shots. Running footsteps.

Capp veered to deeper darkness, to sloping ground that gave way damply beneath his faltering steps. He was running crouched low, pain gnawing frenziedly at him. Both of his sleeves, his hands, were darker than the night, and his breath came in whistling desperate spasms of agony. Chereno was still after him, along with the Secret Service, and Chereno if no one else was still firing as Capp made his way along a low hedge toward the back of the building.

There was blood in Capp's throat, and he was terrified. He spat out the blood and kept running, feeling more blood well up into his throat. He had given up any hope of escape and wanted only to be taken alive by the Secret Service so he could reveal what he knew about Lazarus. He spat out more blood and tried to cry out his surrender as he ran, but the increasing pain made it impossible to shout.

Weakening, losing blood rapidly, he stumbled on through the darkness, falling to his knees, rising, lurching on. He stepped then where there was nothing and felt himself pitch forward, flashing pain slicing into his knee, a rhythmic pounding on his shoulder and the right side of his face.

Capp was too dazed to know he had tumbled down the wooden flight of stairs to the beach. He lay still, half conscious, the firm sandy soil pressed against his back.

He was aware of several dark figures approaching on the run, against the black sky and wash of steady rain. It was odd that he felt no compulsion to blink as the rain struck his open eyes.

Capp realized that the figures were Secret Service agents. Chereno would be among them but wouldn't dare shoot the now obviously helpless quarry.

The dark figures gathered around, bent over Capp as if in concern, their guns steadily pointing like the operating instruments of compassionate surgeons. The sound of their rasping breath, somehow out of unison with Capp's own, filled the night.

"Bastard!" one of them gasped.

"How did you do it?" another asked shrilly. "How did you get past our security ring?"

Capp raised his head. He struggled to speak, tensing his stomach muscles to force the words out where they could be heard by the proper ears, regarded with the proper alarm. Irony assailed him: silent for so long, and now attempting so desperately to speak, he was unable to do so.

Something seemed to burst deep in his chest and blood welled warmly and thickly again into his throat. He tried to call his wife's name but that was impossible.

He began to choke, and he knew that he couldn't stop choking.

"That's that," he heard someone say with disappointed finality and without the slightest hint of awe.

They stood silently and watched the mad patterns traced by his feet in the sand.

☒ 40

Within twenty minutes the scene was photographed and the doctor arrived to pronounce Capp dead. The body was removed under guard, wrapped in a rubberized sheet, and driven in an escorted white ambulance to nearby Dade Memorial Hospital for autopsy. The press had arrived but was being held at bay outside the grounds. Half of them remained standing in the rain outside the main gate, the other half followed the ambulance.

Andrew Berwin sat behind his desk in his office. Chief Secret Service agent Art Rapaport, wearing a tired but unconcerned expression, sat to the left of the desk. Chereno sat to the right, nearer Berwin. A sheet of plastic had been taped over the shattered window to keep out the rain. Rapaport, whose superiors were on their way by plane from Washington, was questioning the two men according to procedure, while events were still vivid in their minds.

"Apparently he didn't know I was in the office," Chereno was saying. "He burst in here, made as if to reach for a weapon, and I drew my firearm. When he saw me he fumbled again for his weapon, then must have panicked. By that time I was between him and the door. He shouted something and leaped for the window."

"He was armed," Rapaport confirmed, jotting notes in a leather-covered writing pad. With Berwin's permission, the conversation also was being recorded.

"There can be no doubt as to why he came here," Berwin said. "I'm sure we'll find that his prison ordeal had tragically deranged him, that he's responsible for those other deaths. He was always . . . well, abnormal. I believe I'm on record as having said that years ago."

Rapaport continued to write, the pencil held firmly in his long pale fingers. The cassette of the voice-activated recorder on the desk was still.

The rain lessened, then stopped, and in the wake of what had happened the office was suddenly, eerily silent.

"Listen! . . ." Berwin said softly. His stiff features were tense with concentration, eyes focused to one side. "I hear a ticking. Do you hear it? I'm sure . . ."

Rapaport stopped writing and cocked his head, frowned.

Then he sat back, somewhat relieved. "From over there." He motioned casually with his pencil. "It's coming from Mr. Chereno's coat."

Mr. Chereno's coat.

Chereno and Berwin looked at each other. Berwin began a shrill scream. All three men started to stand before an unfolding pure white brilliance.

The entire west wing of the rambling building was destroyed by the blast.

In the explosion's resonant aftermath, dozens of gulls circled in the clearing sky, screaming their puzzlement and outrage, understanding denied them.

☒ EPILOGUE

THE SUN WAS SHINING in Manhattan.

Senator Adam Haller sat at his gray metal desk in his campaign headquarters on Park Avenue South, watching through the poster-cluttered window the noonday stream of pedestrians and madly darting yellow cabs. From the next room came the occasional ring of a telephone that was answered by one of half a dozen young volunteers, and an occasional peal of high, feminine laughter. The atmosphere around the headquarters was easy and informal; this was the camp of the almost certain winner.

Haller caught sight of a car plastered with red, white and blue bumper stickers bearing his name, but he hardly noticed. He was still digesting the news of Andrew Berwin's death, feeling cautiously hopeful, tentatively, joyously unburdened.

Could it really have happened? To reassure himself he again scanned the glaring black headlines of the *Times* on his desk. And it was true; wasn't everything the *Times* printed true?

The possessive, inhibiting power that had propelled Haller to his present height was suddenly gone, leaving him that rarest of political candidates, his own man. A sense of unbridled optimism, of glittering destiny, coursed through him. He hadn't felt this way since his youth. So much was possible. So much. Unfettered, undebted, a Haller administration might well find a Camelot within reach.

Haller sat forward and tried to read over the speech he was to deliver tomorrow at the rally in Teaneck, New Jersey, but he found that he couldn't concentrate. He shook off the impulse to give way to wild, exhilarating laughter.

Gloria, one of the older volunteers, in charge of the phone room, knocked twice and poked her gray-flecked head into the office. "A call for you personally," she said. "No name, but he says it's important and concerns Andrew Berwin. Want to take it?"

Haller knew Gloria had a sixth sense about which telephone calls actually were important enough to bring to his attention. He nodded.

"I'll put it on four one six," Gloria said, and withdrew, closing the door.

With a vague sense of misgiving, he lifted the receiver and pressed the illuminated button.

"Senator Haller?"

"Yes."

"Dwayne Stauker, Senator."

Slowly, immutably, something began to crumble inside Haller.

"How can I help you, Mr. Stauker?"

"I'd like to speak with you privately, Senator. It concerns a matter vital to your career, your future, the country's future . . ."

Outside, just a few feet away on Park Avenue, preoccupied, unknowing, the people streamed past.